DESOLATION

DESOLATION

A Novel

by R *Lawson Gamble*

Zack Tolliver, FBI, Series Book Eleven

R Lawson Gamble Books Imprint
Rich Gamble Associates
Los Alamos, CA

DESOLATION

R LAWSON GAMBLE BOOKS

Cover by KRYSTALYNN DESIGNS

ISBN: 9798988410508 Rich Gamble Associates

For my son Matthew who may one day work in Boron Valley.

The author gratefully acknowledges the assistant of readers Craig and Pamela for their expertise.

DESOLATION

(desolation: a state of complete emptiness or destruction)

TOMESHA

("ground afire" Timbisha Shoshone for Death Valley)

"When shall the stars be blown out of the sky like the sparks blown out of a smithy, and die?"...William Butler Yeats

CHAPTER ONE

The body was deep in the debris-ladened sand that washed over it and solidified like a frozen ocean wave. The surface had then eroded as the flood waters drained, just enough to reveal the top of a head and the fingers of one hand projecting above the surface conglomerate baked hard by the sun. The fingers appeared strangely disassociated from the head, like four pale tubers from some rare desert plant that gestated for decades until brought to life by the once-in-a-century rainfall event. The top of the head was completely bald and might have gone unnoticed as one of many rounded stones dislodged by the flow but for its unusual texture and the strange manner in which it reflected the sun.

Ranger Jim McDowell wasn't there looking for bodies. He was there to assess the damage to the Desolation Canyon Trail from the rushing waters and to calculate the time and resources necessary to reconstruct it. The ranger had just scrambled up the eight-foot fall, less precipitous now thanks to the debris collected there, and was approaching the six-foot fall when the stark white rounded stone caught his eye. Curious, he leaned down to pick it up when something about its surface held him back. Then he noticed the four pale, slender shoots growing out of the sand nearby and, in a flash of horror and nausea, realized they were fingers.

His mind numb, he radioed the office and reported his find. Then he sat down to wait. As he crunched on a nutrition bar, he tried not to think about the body entombed next to him.

The heat and silence conspired to effect drowsiness, and despite the circumstances, his head had begun to droop when the distant chainsaw growl of a quad alerted him. He remained seated, fanning his sweaty face with his hat. He knew the vehicle could come no further than the eight-foot fall, and it would take another ten minutes to pack tools and hike up to his position.

When, at last, they strode into view around a bend in the arroyo, he identified the tall figure of Superintendent Mike Scala. As they came closer, he recognized Melissa Mongrin, a fellow ranger whose expertise was archaeology and anthropology. With a shudder, he realized why the superintendent had chosen to bring her along. What they must do amounted to an archaeological dig.

Mike Scala was the twin of the ATV he had ridden in on; rugged, capable, and loud. His conversation began while he was still twenty yards away.

"A dead man, Mac? Really? I've got ten million in damages from this storm already, and now you say I got a dead man?"

McDowell waited until his grim-faced boss had come close before responding.

"All I can tell you for sure is you have a head and a hand," he said.

Scala surveyed the rock-studded terrain. "Where? Where's the dead man, Mac?"

McDowell pointed. "There."

Scala's eyes widened as they focused on the white pate. "Holy shit!"

Melissa shrugged off her pack and peered down at the submerged head. She pushed a finger down on the hardened sand. "It won't be easy digging him out. It'll take time." She sounded grim, but McDowell noticed her eyes gleamed at the prospect.

Scala was studying the arroyo upstream where it led into the deepening canyon. The dry bed was littered with debris flushed out by the raging waters. Displaced boulders the size of small cars gave witness to the power of the flood.

"The poor bastard never stood a chance," he said.

"I'm wondering what he was doing here," McDowell said. "All the trails were closed, and the warning signs were up. I can't think of a worse place to take a walk during a storm."

Scala sounded defensive. "That's all we can do, you know; warn people and put up signs. After that, it's up to them." He raised a bushy brow, looking at McDowell. "You've been at this job long enough to know people just do what they want to do."

The sound of scraping drew their attention back to the immediate situation. Melissa had her trowel in hand and was tentatively scratching away the sand layer near the gleaming cranium.

"Waddaya think?" Scala asked.

Melissa responded over her shoulder without stopping work. "This upper layer is like concrete, but it should soften as I work deeper."

A moment later, she stood and stretched. "I think he's lying on his back at a forty-five-degree angle, legs three feet below where I'm standing, unless they are doubled back under him. We can use the shovels down at this end to take away the first foot or so." She scraped out a semi-circular groove in the sand. "Dig in here, but go easy; we don't want to perform an accidental amputation."

Scala produced a short shovel from his pack, tossed it to McDowell, and the ranger started to dig. His shovel blade contacted firm objects occasionally, rocks and wood debris, each time causing him to wince, but soon he had dug a hole a foot and a half deep.

Melissa stopped him then and using her trowel, dislodged chunky portions of the top sand layer, working up toward the head. When she was about eight inches from it, the final chunk broke off and slid away, and the loose sand covering the head sifted downward. Now Melissa was staring at a face, its mouth still buried, its eyes open but full of sand, giving it the blank, impersonal look of a sculpture. In the middle of the forehead was a perfectly round hole with a thin cover of sand.

Her gasp brought Scala down to look.

"Dang it! This just became complicated."

"What is it?" McDowell asked, crowding in.

"He's been shot," Melissa whispered.

They were shocked into stillness, a frieze against the sun-drenched sand background, Melissa on her knees still holding her trowel, the two rangers standing above her like shepherds in a manger scene. Then Melissa lifted her trowel to remove the sand still covering the bottom of the face.

"Stop!" Scala ordered. "This is a crime scene now. We can't touch another thing. I need to get orders."

He took out his phone and placed a call. The two rangers watched as he spoke into it.

"I need to speak to Director Jax, please. This is Superintendent Scala...Yes, it's important. We have a body. A man's been shot...Oh, hello, Jock, this is Mike Scala. We've just uncovered a body with a bullet hole in the forehead."

The conversation lasted several minutes after that, with Scala doing a lot of listening and muttering, "Yes, Sir." He eventually pulled the phone from his ear and sighed.

"Director Jax will call for a Special Services Agent, but he has no idea how long it will take for one to get out here. Meanwhile, we need to secure this site and contact local law enforcement. Melissa, you can excavate this body enough so that the detectives can work with it, but be careful not to touch any part of it or any objects you may find that could be considered evidence. Leave those in situ. Clear?"

Melissa nodded.

"Mac, you come with me to the ATV. There's a tarp and some stakes in it you can use to cover the body until the detectives get here. I think we may have a roll of crime tape there."

"What will you do, Mike?" McDowell asked.

"Everything I can to keep people away from this place and stop rumors from spreading."

By the time Mac returned with the tarp and stakes, Melissa had uncovered the lower portion of the face and was excavating under the chin. The mouth was open but filled with sand. Melissa had left it alone in adherence to Mike's order. To Mac, the sand-filled eyes and mouth on the pale white face looked like a rendition of The Scream.

Melissa worked efficiently and accurately, following the right arm to the fingers, then around the collarbone and shoulders. She found the left arm positioned along the side and worked down the torso and arm simultaneously.

"He wasn't wearing a shirt," she remarked without looking back at Mac.

"Maybe it was torn off him by the force of the water," Mac said.

Melissa shook her head. "I don't think so." She stopped and rested back on her haunches, pointing with the trowel. "I'm not seeing the bruises and scrapes I expected to see following a battering from being washed a long way by the flood."

"What do you think that means?"

Melissa shook her head. "It's early days, but I'm beginning to wonder if he was washed down here by the flood waters after all."

"What else could it be?" Mac asked.

Melissa shook her head and went back to work with her trowel.

The heat shimmered. A gnat buzzed Mac's ear, and he swatted at it. Multiple efforts to wipe sweat from his brow had left sandy grit on his forehead. Large sweat patches had grown under the arms of his uniform shirt. He wondered at Melissa, on her knees, stretched forward with arched back over the growing sand cavity, yet apparently oblivious to the heat.

She sat back again. "He's naked," she said. "He has no clothing on at all."

Mac peaked around her at the corpse. Melissa had now uncovered the entire torso and the top portion of the pelvic area. Despite the thin sand layer remaining on the skin surface, he saw she was right. No pants, no belt, no nothing.

"What does it mean?" Mac asked.

Melissa looked unsure for the first time, staring back at Mac. "Maybe it means that the flood didn't bury him; it unburied him."

CHAPTER TWO

Command Chief Simon Barroff gave the paper on his desk an irritated tap with his forefinger. He looked again at the original notification date, then picked up his phone.

"Master Chief, why am I receiving this report of a missing civilian thirty-six hours after the fact?"

There was momentary hesitation at the other end of the line. "Uh, sir, it came to my attention just this morning."

"It says here the missing person was a civilian assigned to Chief Petty Officer Dally. Why was this civilian on the base, and why don't I know about it?"

"He's a fuel expert, apparently, sir. Some admiral from the Yard sent him to help with the X27 project."

Barroff groaned. "What's his clearance?"

"Top drawer, sir, from the Admiral at the Yard."

"Which Admiral?"

Hesitation. "I don't know, sir."

"And again, Master Chief, why the delay?"

"No one realized he was missing until now, sir."

"Yet the Chief Petty Officer realized it when he submitted this report four days ago."

"Yes, sir. It got held up along the line of command in the belief that he would turn up. Civilians are squirrely, Sir, if you know what I mean. They tend to miss checks."

"That doesn't cut the mustard, Master Chief. You will backcheck this situation. I want to know everything about this civilian, who he is, what he was doing here, who is the admiral who authorized him, why I wasn't informed, and most of all, where the hell he is right now! On the double!"

=

Chief Petty Officer Burk Dally's big hand shook when he hoisted his coffee mug. He hadn't slept worth a crap the last several days. Who could sleep with a shitstorm of this size looming over his head?

He set the cup down on the metal table top in the canteen before anyone could notice the quivering. His thoughts returned for the millionth time to the morning Dr. Helmut Sweiger had entered his facility, briefcase in hand, dressed as if for an Easter Sunday church service in a two-piece suit and wearing a supercilious smile.

Dr. Sweiger's escort had handed Burk the orders. The man was a fuel expert, was to be given every consideration, would help them through the oxidation impasse they were experiencing, blah blah blah, on the authority of some admiral.

So Burk showed him to the lab and introduced the team. They'd begun to brief him, walk him through their research, and show him the problems, but he wouldn't listen. He'd held up his palm like a goddam Caesar, taken over the computer console, and begun reading it for himself. A real team guy. Burk had felt the team's eyes on him, but all he could do was shrug and walk away.

Two hours later, he learned Helmut the Magnificent had left the lab building, somehow requisitioned a vehicle, and driven down range into the desert wearing a Sunday suit, for Christ's sake, oblivious to any unexploded ordinance or current test firing schedules or any other damn thing. And then he'd managed to disappear completely.

Burk had known right away this was trouble, real trouble. He'd immediately sent security out to find him and bring him back. But they never found him.

They found the vehicle though, hours later, left with its keys in it near the motor pool, but no Sweiger. They figured he'd got lost somewhere on the base trying to find his way back to the lab building. Security put out an all-eyes alert, but nobody was particularly alarmed, guessing he'd turn up. But Burk, a seasoned Navy man, sent his report up the chain anyway, more of a CYA kind of thing. He was sure glad of it now; the man never did turn up.

His phone rang. He groaned. He didn't have to look at the caller ID to know who it was.

"Yes, sir?"

He listened to a five-minute stream of curt, precise words.

"The admiral's name was Tyrone, sir, Admiral Tyrone," he said. "The orders were on his official letterhead. I have the copy, sir."

He listened again. "Yes, sir, I will sir. Thank you, sir."

Burk wiped the sweat from his forehead after he put away his phone. The shitstorm was full-blown now. They'd comb the entire base for the missing man, inch by inch. And it would not be easy. The China Lake Naval Weapons

Center sat in the middle of 1.1 million acres of the Western Mojave Desert, an area larger than the state of Rhode Island. Farther north and east was the even less hospitable landscape of Death Valley. If they didn't find Helmut the Magnificent among the buildings of the base, he was almost certainly toast.

=

Command Chief Simon Barroff placed a call to Admiral Tippy Tyrone at the Naval Sea Systems Command at the Yard, Washington D.C.. He knew Tippy. They'd come up through the Naval Academy together. That made this call a little easier.

"Simon, it's good to hear from you. Did you receive my surprise gift?"

"I suspect so, Tippy. That's why I'm calling you."

"No thanks are necessary, old friend. None at all. The man crossed my bow at a gathering recently and I thought, why, this is just what my buddy Simon needs to solve his little oxidation problem. So I was able to arrange it, got the man on loan. The guy's a genius, I'm told, a complete wizard."

"I don't know how to say this, sir, so I'll just flat-out tell you. We lost him."

The phone went silent. "Simon, what do you mean you lost him?"

"He's gone. We can't find him. An hour after he arrived, he walked out of the lab, obtained a vehicle, and drove down the east range. His vehicle returned, but he's been missing ever since. We're scouring the facility."

"Simon, this is serious. This is F.U.B.A.R.."

"I know, I know, we're balls to the walls here. If he's wandering around the base anywhere, we'll find him. But if he's still out on the range somewhere..."

"Listen, Simon, you've got to nuke it out. Find this guy." Tippy's voice dropped to a whisper. "Dead or alive, Simon. We need a body. This man's got stuff in his head that can't get out. We need to know where he is or was. If he talks to the wrong people...well, we won't even go there. Find him, Simon!"

"But we're in the middle of a desert. No one—"

"Find him!"

The call ended.

CHAPTER THREE

"How long ago did he go missing?" Zack asked. They waited for the pretty young Navajo girl to clear their dinner plates.

"Three days ago," Eagle Feather said after the waitress bustled off.

Zack was about to remark that the prospect of finding traces of a man traveling across blowing sand three days ago was slim until he remembered how many times the Navajo guide sitting across from him had done precisely that in the past, and instead asked, "Is the pay good?"

If I can track him, yes."

"If not?"

Eagle Feather turned a curious gaze on Zack. "It is interesting. They wish to know more about where he has been than where he is now."

He turned the conversation back to Zack. "Any new cases?"

Zack grinned. "Nothing official. I'm helping Jimmy sort out some Skinwalker sightings."

"Ho! Helping the Navajo Nation Police, revisiting your early FBI days. You have learned some things since then."

Zack nodded, looking sheepish. "One or two, I guess. The Elk Wells Navajo Police Station is stretched thin right now, and they don't have the manpower to investigate the sightings, so as head of the department, Jimmy felt he had to take it upon himself. I'm just giving him a hand."

He cocked his head at Eagle Feather. "When do you leave?"

"As soon as I finish my dessert."

=

Zack thought over Eagle Feather's words as he walked away from Katie's Cafe. It was unusual for the U.S. Armed Services, particularly the Navy, to hire a civilian to track a man across the desert. You'd expect they'd turn to their special-skills units, like the Seals. Of course, Eagle Feather was the best, and his reputation was widespread. Still, there must be other reasons to go outside the Navy. Secrecy, maybe? Was it something they didn't want anyone in the chain of command to know about?

He chuckled, picturing Eagle Feather in his black leather vest and pants, the old reservation hat with the single limp feather, among the prim and proper uniformed Navy officers. He'd give anything to be there.

His phone sounded with his boss Janice's ringtone. Zack pulled to the side of the road to answer it.

"Good morning, Zack. I have a case for you."

"Okay...?" These moments induced a certain amount of anxiety.

"A body has been found in Death Valley National Park. The ISB special agent could use some help."

"ISB?"

"Investigative Services Branch."

"Why me?"

"Not for the usual reasons," she said.

The department Zack headed was Janice Hooper's unique creation within the FBI, a unit specializing in cultural differences, mysticism, and apparent paranormal cases—basically, everything other agents did not want. Too often, Janice turned to him when other agents were simply too busy, to Zack's mind.

"Okay...?"

"This body might have been washed from somewhere up Desolation Canyon by the recent flooding. The body is naked. There is nothing to identify it.

"Okay..."

"Cause of death was a single bullet through the head by a high-power rifle at long range. Do I have your full attention now?"

"You do." She did.

The long rifle was the specialty of Maria, the assassin. Ever since the contests between them, any case involving a sniper sparked Zack's interest. And Janet knew it.

He heard a soft chuckle. "The investigation is being conducted from Furnace Creek. I'm sending all the information you'll need. When can you be there?"

Zack looked at his watch. "Where is the closest airfield to Furnace Creek?"

"Right there. Furnace Creek has an airfield for small planes."

"I'll be there by eight tonight."

=

Libby was out in the field working her dogs when Zack arrived home. She gave a big wave as his Jeep turned in the drive, then returned to her work. She trained scent dogs, an occupation that often went hand in glove with Zack's career. A sniffer dog might well come in handy in this case, Zack thought.

He went directly to his office and his computer. He accessed his FBI site and opened the file placed there by Janice. In it were the first-hand observations by a ranger named Melissa Mongrin, a specialist in archaeology and paleontology. She had unearthed the body from the water-swept sand. She'd had to treat the exhumation like an archaeological dig, painstakingly unearthing the body with a trowel. She'd discovered the body was naked, that there was a bullet hole in the forehead, and observed a lack of any bruising or other trauma to the body, suggesting that the man had been dead when the water torrents engaged him.

The Inyo County Coroner's office had verified death by a gunshot from a distance greater than a hundred yards, citing lack of powder burns or residue on the victim's skin, along with the amount of exit damage from the bullet to the back of the head. They'd not found the bullet nor any other evidence near the body. They speculated the body had not traveled far, given the force of the waters roaring down the canyon, which would have damaged the body over a longer distance, perhaps even severing limbs.

A report from the ISB special agent, Trisha Knolls, stated she had searched for the original burial site but failed to find it. She was currently examining park registers and interviewing rangers to try to identify the body, but given the multiplicity of possible entry points to the park, official or otherwise, she realized it was a long shot. Visitation to the park had been down as many attractions were still closed. Trisha was now searching through missing person files.

Zack pondered the information in the file. There was a sketch of the face which included the bullet hole. The placement of the bullet had been precise, directly above the ridge of the nose. It was an expert shot from any distance greater than that cited by the coroner or a lucky one. And there had been no follow-up shot, again suggesting an economy usually exhibited by professionals sure of their skills.

Zack felt a mix of excitement and dread. *Whoa, boy, there are many skilled snipers out there besides Maria*, he told himself, but he reached for the phone and arranged a flight from the Tuba City Airport to Furnace Creek for six p.m. that evening.

Now to tell Libby.

CHAPTER FOUR

The call came while Zack stood on the tarmac at the Tuba City Airport, watching the pilot do his preflight inspection. Every time he visited this tiny airfield, his mind flashed images of his first arrival as a wet-behind-the-ears recruit. The barren red-earthed landscape, leading his eyes to distant mesa cliffs, half-shadowed by fading evening light, was the same, but for some additional billboards meant for airplane passengers. There were improvements to the tiny terminal and new buildings, but the sense of timelessness and his insignificance within the mammoth scale of this landscape still overpowered him.

He lifted the phone to his ear. It was Janice.

"Change in plans, Zack," she said. "I need you to change your flight."

"What's going on, Janice?"

"I need you to make a deposition before a federal judge in San Diego. Right now. There's a termination time on this order. I don't want this mess going public."

Zack hesitated. "What mess?"

"Your theft of a taco truck outside the naval hospital a couple of years ago."

Zack remembered it well. "Jesus, Janice, I was running for my life. I thought you had settled that. Wasn't the driver reimbursed?"

"More than amply. We have a signed affidavit to that effect and a signed no-harm document. But apparently, the driver changed his mind, and now the court order has been issued."

"What about this Death Valley case?"

"It'll keep until you can get up there. The deposition won't take long. We've forwarded all the necessary documents to the Federal Court in San Diego. Everything will be there when you appear. But you have to go in person—right now. Go, make your deposition, then fly directly up to Furnace Creek."

Zack was not happy. "This will mean at least a twenty-four-hour delay on the case. You know what that can mean sometimes. It's already been days since they found the body."

"It can't be helped, Zack."

Zack went to the pilot and told him about the change in plans. The man shrugged and called his charter company, then went to file a new flight plan. Zack went to the terminal to wait. He read through his file on the Death Valley case, hoping to put this time to good use.

It was another hour before the pilot was ready. The flight to San Diego was uneventful. The court offices were closed for the day, so Zack made an appointment online for first thing in the morning.

Janice had booked a nice room for him in the Hilton, her way of apologizing, Zack figured. He shrugged, billed a nice meal to the department, chatted with Libby over the phone, and went to bed early.

He woke at six and was at the courthouse in plenty of time for his nine a.m. deposition. When he entered the courtroom, he recognized the taco truck driver. He was surprised to see him, expecting he would sign a document, not engage in a hearing.

The judge addressed Zack.

"Good morning, Agent Tolliver. It seems we owe you an apology. According to this man, whose name was on the complaint, he intends no such action."

Zack raised an eyebrow but said nothing.

The judge turned to the truck owner. "Mr. Ramirez, do you want to withdraw your complaint?"

The man looked puzzled. "I can't withdraw a complaint I never made," he said.

"Are you, or are you not represented by the firm Matthews, Jorgenson, and Bitty?"

The man shook his head. "No, Your Honor, I never heard of them."

"Mr. Ramirez, know that you are under oath. Perjury is a serious matter."

"Your Honor, I say again, I never made a complaint and never heard of that Matthews and whatever law firm."

The judge sat in silent irritation, staring at the Taco truck driver. Then she turned her gaze on Zack.

"Again, Agent Tolliver, we apologize for wasting your time. We will investigate this false complaint. You may go."

She looked back at the taco truck driver. "Mr. Ramirez, please remain if you wouldn't mind. We need to ask you a few more questions and try to sort this out."

Zack left the courtroom, his phone in his hand, and pressed the number for the charter pilot, who had remained in San Diego overnight. He assured Zack he'd be ready to take off as soon as Zack could get to the airport. Regardless, it was another hour before Zack was seated, belted, and waiting for the plane to take off.

The engine roared, and the small plane began to move. Almost immediately, it lurched and came to a stop. Zack saw they were still on an access apron and not in a queue. The pilot came back a moment later.

"Bad news," he said. "We've lost inflation in a tire. We have to wait for repairs."

"I thought you'd done your preflight check," Zack said.

The pilot grimaced. "I did. Both tires are relatively new and in fine shape, or so I thought. I'm going to take a look."

"I'll come with you," Zack said.

Once they were out of the plane, the problem was obvious. The tire on the right landing gear was flat. Zack went for a closer look. As the pilot had said, the tire looked new, and the tread was hardly worn.

"Could there have been something on the tarmac that could slice into the tire?"

The pilot shook his head in doubt. "Anything's possible, but it's unlikely. These tires are built tough. They have Kevlar strips and inflate to six times the pressure of car tires. I've never had this happen before."

Zack saw an airport tow truck approaching. "That was quick!"

"They don't want planes sitting out here gumming up the works for very long," the pilot said. "He'll have us up and running quickly. But it's gonna cost the company five hundred bucks!"

"Will you keep the tire?"

The pilot looked at him strangely. "No. The airport keeps it. They'll want to investigate the problem."

"Not this time," Zack said. He called Janice. She was on another line. As he waited, he watched the truck lift the small plane by the landing strut and watched the mechanic begin to remove the wheel.

"Hi, Zack. Have you made your deposition?"

"None was necessary," Zack said and explained the situation. "And now I'm waiting for a blown tire on the plane to be changed. God knows how long before we return to the takeoff queue again."

"You say there was no complaint? Just some mistake?"

"I'm beginning to wonder if it was a mistake," Zack said. "Or if this blown tire was truly just a freak accident. Janice, I want this tire examined by our people."

He could almost hear Janice's brain whirring.

"Give your phone to the repairman," she said.

Zack did.

The man listened. Zack saw his face register surprise. Then he said "Yes, ma'am," several times and returned the phone to Zack.

"I've made the arrangements," Janice said. "Enjoy your flight."

CHAPTER FIVE

Eagle Feather's task was simple; to track a man across a naval firing range and either find him or report where he had gone. For this, he would receive a nice sum of money and the eternal gratitude of the Navy, or more likely, the thanks of the commanding officer, whose ass was on the line. But in the end, it didn't matter. You can't spend gratitude.

He'd been issued an ATV for the task, packed full of water, provisions, and survival gear that he knew he would never need. The firing range was huge, at 16,600 square miles, the largest in the U.S., absorbing a big chunk of the Western Mojave desert, where only feral horses, feral burros, bighorn sheep, and the endangered desert tortoise lived. Somewhere out there, a specialist in propulsion fuels from Washington D.C. had gone off in a Humvee and disappeared, yet somehow his vehicle had returned home.

Previous investigators from the Navy had begun with the assumption that if the vehicle had returned, so must the driver. That assumption had led nowhere.

Eagle Feather learned that no one had driven the vehicle since the disappearance, a bit of unusual foresight or probably just luck. He examined it closely, scraped out the soil layers embedded deep in the large tire treads, examined each tire, checked the undercarriage for oil or hydraulic fluid leaks, and compared the mileage in the vehicle with its log from before and after the event.

The Petty Officer Second Class, who had issued the vehicle to the civilian, now demoted to Seaman, said the man had asked him how to operate the GPS unit, then had asked for directions to the eastern ranges. He had guessed that the man had a specific location in mind.

With this in mind, Eagle Feather drove from pavement to graded dirt to ruts, always heading east. Once off the pavement, there was a chaotic and overwhelming network of tracks from many vehicles. But Eagle Feather searched for one particular irregularity he'd noticed on the right rear tire of the Humvee, studying each set of tire tracks that departed from the system of ruts and eliminating them one by one. It was tedious work and demanded patience, a trait the Navajo hunting guide possessed in spades.

The sun's glare from the reflecting sands was blinding, and the temperature was gasping above 110 degrees when Eagle Feather finally found what he sought, the broad track of a Humvee tire exhibiting a slight transverse indentation where a narrow ridge of excess rubber left on the molded tire surface during production imprinted into the sand. It was so insignificant as to be unnoticed by anyone not expecting to see it. The vehicle tracks led off from the main ruts in a northerly direction.

Several other vehicles had turned this way over time, but before long, his Humvee turned east, leaving the other tracks, its tire prints in the sand disappearing into the sun's glint like the shining rails of a train track.

Eagle Feather paused to study prints of Google Earth terrain pictures he'd scanned of the area. Although there were large swaths of blacked-out terrain, areas the Navy had secured from view, there was enough remaining for Eagle Feather to establish his location.

He oriented himself to a pair of distant hills rising above the flats in the direction the Humvee tracks headed. He found a matching satellite picture and studied it. He saw that the higher elevations marked an area of general uplift severed by deep arroyos. It looked like rough country where even the Humvee might find travel difficult.

Eagle Feather made good progress on the flats, and the distant hills grew closer, revealing details of vegetation patches, rock formations, and fissures. The Humvee tracks led straight toward a narrow cleft between two ridgelines.

But as he neared, Eagle Feather realized the apparent gap between the two hills was not the easy passage it promised from afar. House-sized chunks of sandstone thrust up at odd angles within it, skirted by steep sand ridges. Here the Humvee had ended its outward journey. Deep troughs in the sand showed where the vehicle had spun its wheels. It had then backed out and traveled away along the foot of the hills, back toward the base. Next to the tire troughs were two sets of footprints that tracked up the steep sand slope.

Eagle Feather left his ATV and went for a closer look. He saw that the footprints were from different people traveling in opposite directions. The larger size feet, those of the scientist, had exited the Humvee. Occasional indentations along his tracks showed where his hands had gone into the sand in the struggle to climb. His prints had not returned. The smaller footprints traveled down the slope, entered the Humvee, and drove away. The Humvee tire tracks would no doubt lead back to the base. Eagle Feather now focused on where the scientist had gone.

Beyond the top of the sand ridge, the ground sloped away, passing between guardian sandstone formations. Here, where funneled winds had swept over the sand, the surface was firm, and footprints less distinct, requiring more of Eagle Feather's attention. It was clear to the Navajo that Small Foot was backtracking the scientist, leaving as few prints as possible. In areas of windswept sandstone, where impressions were all but invisible, he searched for the scientist's heavier tracks, knowing the backtracker would have passed that way.

The hunt led him down to a low hollow among barren hills. The sand was deep here, having drifted from the slopes of the surrounding hills. The scientist's tracks came to an abrupt end.

Eagle Feather retraced his steps to the last of the scientist's footprints. These were clear and firm, the forefoot depth indicating no change in pace. Then– nothing. A short distance away, he found prints by Small Foot that appeared from nowhere, moving in the opposite direction.

The Navajo knelt by the final print and studied the ground beyond it. The sand there appeared natural, undisturbed, with small wind-sculpted ridges and a slight dusting of leaves and debris. He concentrated on a six-inch square area a single stride beyond the final footprint but saw nothing. He reached out with the tip of a finger and began lightly brushing sand away, a few grains at a time. It flicked away at first, and then it didn't. Beneath, the sand was solid. As he dug deeper, his finger found a firm edge. He grunted in satisfaction and continued brushing with infinite care until he had exposed a footprint.

Eagle Feather rocked back on his haunches and studied it. It was as if the man had descended beneath the sand. The footprints continued, but how far?

To answer that question, the Navajo traversed the side of the hill above the hollow. On the opposite side of the pocket of loose sand, he found just a trace of a print. Here the surface was firm, and the indications slight, but the Navajo's trained eye saw that Small Foot had come down the slope toward the deep sand from somewhere beyond.

But the footprints of the scientist had never left the deep sand.

CHAPTER SIX

Zack's plane landed on the small airfield at Furnace Creek without further incident. He had called ahead and, glancing out of the airplane window, saw a woman leaning against a National Park Dodge Ram pickup truck.

Zack waited for the pilot to unlatch the door, then climbed to the tarmac. It had been unseasonably warm in San Diego, but now Zack faced a sudden blast of heat like a curtain of molten lava. The pilot handed down his carry-on, touched his cap, and closed the door. The plane began to taxi away the moment Zack was clear.

The woman he had seen by the truck strode toward him. She wore a bush shirt with ventilating flaps and lightweight cargo pants. Under her wide-brimmed hat, Zack saw a tanned, youthful face with startling blue eyes framed by short blonde hair.

Her handshake was firm.

"Welcome, Agent Tolliver. Tisha Knolls. I hope your trip was pleasant." White teeth gleamed, and her eyes crinkled pleasantly.

Zack gave a lop-sided grin. "It was not without its moments," he said. "Thank you for meeting me." He waved an arm in the air indicating the heat. "I guess I'll need to get used to this."

Tisha's smile was sympathetic. "It's expected to heat up a bit more later today. Would you like to go to your quarters first or get right to work?"

"Where can I buy you a soda while you tell me where we stand?"

"Right this way." She began walking, and Zack went with her. Her stride was long and purposeful.

Zack noticed how the clarity of the air brought the distant tall mountains into sharp relief, so much so that he felt he could almost touch them.

"Have you identified the body yet?" he asked.

"No." She glanced up at him from under her hat brim. "The body has no characteristics that can help us; no scars, tattoos, special dental work, former injuries—nothing. We've done massive searches in several databases for missing persons."

"DNA?"

She nodded. "We have it and have just begun searching for matches. Nothing yet."

They were at the truck. Zack slipped into the passenger side of the cab. He noted a thick layer of dust halfway up the white paint. This agent spent time in the field, for sure.

Tisha buckled up and started the truck. As they moved off, she said, "There's a taco place a few miles from the Visitors Center where you can buy me that soda."

"Sounds good to me."

The truck AC blew strong. Zack felt his comfort zone returning. She glanced at him and smiled. "If you're like me, you'll soon find yourself chilled by air-conditioned places. Something about popping in and out of the heat saps my energy."

Zack glanced at her. "What do you do about it?"

She laughed. Zack noticed again how white her teeth showed against the dark tan of her face.

"You'll think me crazy, but I usually drive around with the window open and eat lunches at picnic benches outside."

Zack stared at her. "Yeah, that seems kinda nutty. God invented air conditioning so we wouldn't have to suffer."

She laughed again.

Zack was feeling very comfortable with this woman. It boded well for the progress they must make together.

The buildings of Furnace Creek disappeared behind them, and the flat distances of the valley took their place. Zack took in the vast landscape. A solitary sign with a red arrow advertised Shaved Ice and Indian Fry Bread. As Zack was about to ask who the Indians were, another sign welcomed them to the Timbisha Shoshoni Tribe.

A short time later, Tisha steered the truck into the parking area of a low white building. The sign read Timbisha Tacos.

"Are you hungry?" Tisha asked. "Their burritos are delicious."

Zack felt his stomach growl in response. "I'm ready. Where's the picnic table?"

Tisha plucked the keys out of the ignition. "It's around back. But I won't put you through that right away. Best to acclimatize gradually."

The cafe interior was large and sparsely furnished, with many square-legged cafe tables. Tisha selected one in a corner. As they wended their way to it, they passed a variety of seated customers ranging in appearance from expensive-looking tourists to T-shirt-clad men.

"Are we on a reservation?" Zack asked.

Tisha nodded. "We're on about 7500 acres recognized as the official Timbisha homeland."

"Within the National Park?"

"They were here first. But the Park Service did all they could to move them for decades."

Zack thought about the dead man. "Are there bad feelings?"

Tisha looked taken aback. "You mean between the Park Service and the Timbisha? Not enough to kill a man. These are good people. They'll protest but would never harm anyone. Besides, we have no reason to believe the dead man worked for the National Park Service."

"Just putting a finger to the wind," Zack said. "Have you a theory bout the man's death?"

"I try not to theorize before I have enough facts. It's too easy to skew the evidence toward my theory instead of simply following it." She rose from the table. "I'll go put our order in."

Zack cocked an eye toward her. "You know what I want?"

Her smile was mischievous. "I do."

Zack watched her walk to the counter. He'd worked with agents from the Park Service Investigative Services Branch before, with indifferent results. But this agent seemed confident and well briefed.

He glanced at other tables, catching the quickly averted eyes of some locals. He was pretty sure they'd already spotted him as a G man.

Tisha returned holding two steaming cups and placed one in front of Zack.

"Fresh coffee, as promised." She sat in front of the other cup. "They don't let it burn on a hot plate here, like other places."

Zack sipped. It was delicious.

"So. What are your questions," Tisha asked.

"How did he die?"

"He was shot with a rifle. The bullet entered his brain directly above his nose and blew out the back of his head."

"But not where they found him."

She nodded. "He was killed somewhere else. His clothing and all identifying items—rings, watch, whatever––were stripped from him."

"He'd been buried?"

"That's not certain," Tisha said. "The coroner's people were unable to determine that for sure. We thought at first he'd been washed downstream in a debris flow, so..." She shrugged.

"You've searched upstream?"

She nodded. "As have others. The canyon narrows and deepens, and the debris flow swept everything clean from the headwall down. Any signs that might have been there are long gone."

"Is it possible to tell from the body's condition how far it traveled in the debris flow?"

"That's the question," Tisha said, setting down her cup. "Melissa, the staff archaeologist who unearthed the body, noted very few of the abrasions on it one might expect to find from a body being scraped and sanded over a long distance. That's why she posited soil covered the body not far from where they found it, maybe by backwash."

"Makes sense."

Two large plates of food were traveling toward them in the hands of a young waitress. The young woman set one in front of each of them, along with several small cups of salsa. Each plate contained one huge mix of vegetables and meat wrapped in toasted flatbread.

"This you'll love," Tisha said, and reached for the salsa.

Zack's appetite surged with the delicious aroma. He set to it. A moment later, he sighed and sat back. "How could someone access that canyon area other than by the foot trail?"

"I'll need to show you on a detailed map," Tisha said. "But there is a spur road called Artist's Drive which comes within a quarter mile of the head of Desolation Canyon. It's rough terrain in between, though."

Zack wiped his mouth with a paper napkin. "Could an ATV get there?"

"To get a sniper to a high point overlooking the canyon? Yes. To bring in a body?" She thought about it and shrugged. "I suppose so, although the descent into the canyon would be pretty tough. And why bother? You could drop the body anywhere along the way, and odds are, no one would ever find it." Her gaze was curious. "What are you thinking?"

"I'm not sure. If you stack it all up, you've got a body that, according to the person who unearthed it, had not been swept very far, was naked, with no clothing or personal articles found nearby, and the victim was shot from a distance by an apparent expert. So you ask yourself, did the kill shot come before or after stripping the man? If before, which seems more likely, the killer would have had to approach the body to remove the clothing. But in that scenario, the killer would have had to enter the canyon after shooting the man, remove the clothing, perhaps shovel some dirt over the corpse, and then climb back out of the canyon with the man's clothing and personal items, leaving footprints when descending into the canyon and then when climbing back out again."

"Not necessarily," Tisha said. "Remember, all this had happened before the torrential rains, which washed away any signs the killer."

Zack thought about it.

Tisha gave him a mischievous look. "What explanation can you devise for the second scenario, where the killer removed the clothing first and then shot his victim at long range?"

Zack grinned. "Just one. The victim is captured elsewhere, stripped of his belongings and clothing, bound and gagged, brought to the canyon rim, and then set loose. As he runs down into the canyon, the killer shoots him."

Tisha nodded in appreciation. "Not bad. Just one glitch. The bullet struck the front of his head, not the back."

Zack shrugged. "The man thinks he's a safe distance away, turns to check on the location of his pursuer, and zap! The killer shoots. He then walks away, never having to enter the canyon."

"Leaving his victim lying there in the open?"

Zack's grinned and shrugged. "That part isn't certain yet."

When nothing remained of their burritos but crumbs, they sat back, finishing their coffee.

"What would you like to do first?" Tisha asked. "I can take you back to your accommodations."

"If it's alright, I'd like to visit the scene."

CHAPTER SEVEN

Eagle Feather squatted on the hill summit, staring down at the hollow at the base of the ridge where the deep sand had drifted. From here, a couple of hundred feet above, he saw an area of a slightly darker hue. As he suspected, someone had carefully and skillfully molded the sand back over that area to cover the signs of what had occurred there. He studied the darker patch, orienting its dimensions in his mind with the nearby brush as a reference. Then he came back down the hill to where the prints had disappeared.

Eagle Feather began sifting sand through his fingers. Despite the heat augmented within the confines of the reflective hills surrounding him, the Navajo persisted in his patient search.

An hour passed, and then he felt rather than saw a moist substance that adhered to the sand grains, creating clumps stickier than the dampness from the recent rains. He continued his search and found increasing amounts. At last, he sat back on his haunches. He had found what he had expected: blood—lots of it.

It was a kill site. Smaller Foot had killed Bigger Foot. There was no way to determine the murder method. Any signs in the sand that might have told the story had been wiped clean and then covered, but the blood remained where it had seeped into the sand and congealed. Eagle Feather took a sample and sealed it in a Ziplock baggie. The DNA it contained would confirm the identity of the victim.

His mission was almost complete. He now knew where the fuel expert had gone after he left the base and where his life had ended. He knew where the killer had gone—back to the Humvee. He knew the victim was not at the kill site.

He did not know the location of the body or exactly how he died, for the killer had hidden all evidence of that meeting.

The Navajo began to backtrack the killer to see if he could learn anything more. He crossed the deep sand and followed the smaller imprints up the far slope. At the ridge top, he stopped and scanned the ground on both sides. It had been a planned kill by a professional, most likely a contract hit. The killer had enticed him here in some way, had waited for him to arrive, hidden somewhere near, his method of killing already decided, the cover-up and evacuation of the body already planned.

A rifle would have been his weapon of choice. No one would hear the shot or give it a second thought. The assassin had selected this hollow for the execution. The victim would leave his vehicle due to the terrain and walk to the site, most likely to a GPS location, as the motor pool man had suggested. He would be an easy target for a sniper while walking down the slope toward the sandy hollow.

Eagle Feather thought like a rifleman and looked for a place of concealment that offered the best shot. His eye settled on a hillock above and somewhat behind the sand ridge where a thatch of sage clung to the sandy soil. He went there.

The Navajo did not expect to find any evidence in the crusted sand, nor did he. The killer had been careful. He would not find a discarded shell casing or even a knee imprint. The assassin would have cleaned and groomed the area after the kill shot, and the intervening rains would have done the rest. Eagle Feather went to the brush, studied it, then lay prone, holding an imagined rifle, and squirmed into the best place to sight the ridge where the victim would have appeared. He worked himself into the perfect place. And then, a gift. The Navajo saw a tiny broken twig dangling by its bark sinew from the sage where the rifle barrel must have been.

Eagle Feather stood and stretched. It was time to learn how the killer came to this site. The heavy rains in the interim would have eliminated much of the evidence, but he felt buoyed by his recent success. He walked back down to the sand ridge and studied the ground inch by inch, moving away from the ambush area. He found nothing until he came to an area protected from the west winds by sand hills. There he found a slight indention, then another, no more than tiny lines in the sand. His eye filled in the blanks, and his mind saw footprints walking toward the ambush. Backtracking further, he found more footprints, deeper at the sole and farther apart—running feet that had slowed to a walk. The running feet began at two deep depressions. Beyond them, there was nothing.

Eagle Feather rocked back on his heels and thought about it. There was only one way to read the sequence of prints: the killer had dropped from a height, landing hard, the momentum causing him to run forward a few steps until settling into a walk.

His mission was now complete. The missing scientist had been summoned to this preselected site and killed by a professional assassin. Following the killing, the rifleman had skillfully concealed his presence and all evidence of the murder and then returned the Humvee to the motor pool.

Two mysteries remained: how the killer had reached the area and how the body had disappeared. But all that was beyond his job description. It was time to return to the base and collect his fee.

=

Command Chief Simon Barroff stared at the man dressed all in leather standing before him in a black reservation hat and moccasins and grappled to understand what the man had just told him.

He turned to Chief Petty Officer Dally, who had escorted the Navajo to his office.

"Chief, you told me this man knows his craft."

"Aye, Sir, I had it on good authority. He's the best."

"Yet here he is telling me what we already know—the civilian disappeared."

"Aye, Sir. But he found the location of the disappearance."

"And how does that help us?"

"Sir, we know now that the civilian was decoyed in some way to drive to a specific location out on the range. According to this tracker, the location was an ambush site. It seems to me it indicates conspiracy, Sir."

"You believe someone on the base was involved?"

"It's hard to say, Sir, but it is certainly possible."

Commander Barroff turned to Eagle Feather. "What makes you so sure this man Sweiger is dead?"

The killer shot him with a rifle from two hundred yards," Eagle Feather said. "There was blood. If the killer wanted to capture him, he would have done something different."

"Could he have winged him enough to pacify him?"

"There was too much blood."

Barroff drummed his fingers on his desk, staring at Eagle Feather. "And you say his body is gone? Vanished?"

"His body is not at that location."

"How can you be so sure, with tons of sand and miles of barren desert available to bury him in?"

Eagle Feather met Barroff's eyes. "I am a tracker. The victim never left the ambush site. The ground beneath the deep sand was not disturbed. His body is not there."

"You are telling me Sweiger somehow disappeared from that place. Vanished!"

The Navajo's expression was unchanged. "The killer was the only one to walk away from there."

Barroff's face showed his frustration.

Dally spoke up. "I think Eagle Feather is saying the body did not leave by land, meaning it must have left by air," he said.

"He thinks Sweiger's body was removed by air."

41

Dally looked unhappy. "It seems the only remaining possibility, Sir."

Barroff's eyes swung between the two men. "A helicopter? But even an AH-6 Little Bird would leave some signs of landing."

"Sir, the heavy rains since then could have erased all signs." Dally looked at Eagle Feather for confirmation, but the Navajo remained impassive.

"Well, goddammit, that means someone flew a bird to that location on that day. Check the flight logs, Chief. It's a restricted area. There will be a record."

Dally looked even more miserable. "I've already checked, Sir. There is no record of any aircraft flying there that day, Sir."

Barroff's face reddened. Then he released his breath slowly, and when he spoke next, his voice was calm.

"Any intruding aircraft would have set off alarms. Meaning it had to be one of our own. Also meaning, the flight logs must have been tampered with." Barroff's eyes bore into Dally. "Chief, you will issue this man his fee and escort him off the base. Eagle Feather, the Navy thanks you for your service. That is all, gentlemen."

"Sir, shall I authorize an investigation of the flight logs that day? I—"

"You will stand down, Chief Petty Officer. I will handle it from here. And Chief..."

"Sir?"

Keep this matter confidential. Do you understand?"

"Aye, aye, Sir." Dally saluted, turned on his heel, and escorted Eagle Feather from the room.

Once the door had shut behind them, Barroff reached for his phone.

"Tippy! Simon here. I'm calling to report on the little matter we discussed earlier. Your information is secure."

There was a short silence. "I assume that means the subject no longer exists?"

"Yes, Sir."

"And his whereabouts secured for the time he was with you?"

"Completely."

"Excellent. I trust you will report this as one of the many possible accidents that can occur out on a weapons test range?"

"No problem, Tippy. Unexploded ordinance is all over the area."

"Perfect, Simon. I expect to see you and your lovely wife up here in Washington for a visit someday soon. We have a lot of catching up to do."

CHAPTER EIGHT

When they approached the sign indicating the Desolation Canyon turnoff, Tisha slowed and prepared to turn. Zack stopped her.

"Wait," he said. "I'd like to see where the killer might approach the canyon from Artist's Drive, as you suggested. We can look at the location of the body, but I doubt I'll find anything you haven't already found there."

"Suit yourself," Tisha said and drove on.

They came to the northern terminus of Artist's Drive a short while later, but Tisha continued down the main road.

"It's a one-way loop, " she explained. "We have just under four miles yet to go to our turnoff."

Zack marveled again at the beautiful emptiness of this country with its colorful earth patchwork and etched cliffs.

"I can't imagine traversing this valley by mule," he said. "It must have seemed endless to the pioneers."

Tisha nodded, her eyes on the pitted road. "That's pretty much how Death Valley got its name," she said. "A party of pioneers in the winter of 1849 concluded it would be the death of them. As it turned out, only one of the party did die, but the remaining travelers were very impressed and gave it its name."

Tisha flashed the truck turn signal as they approached the start of Artist's Drive.

"The closest location to Desolation Canyon along this road comes in another four miles," she said as they turned.

The scenery along the drive was magnificent, truly an artist's palette as named. The road climbed and wound amongst rising multicolored hillocks, individually shaded in purple, red, orange, or brown like the separate lumps of paint on an artist's palette.

Several miles later and a short time after the road had looped back toward the west, Tisha pulled the truck to the shoulder, stopped, and turned to Zack.

"The end of the Desolation Canyon trail is about a thousand feet from here as the crow flies. If you are not a crow but want to reach the area between the falls where they found the body, it's close to a half mile climbing over that ridge. But as you can see, that would be very tough going."

She pointed toward a flat area a little behind them. "The only reasonable way to get there, in my opinion, is along that couloir. Although it initially leads to the northeast, it loops back to the west when it bypasses these steep ridges."

Zack raised a brow, eyeing her. "How do you know this landscape so well? You were just assigned here."

She gave a quiet smile. "I've had the same thoughts you had, trying to think as the killer might think. I studied a map. But I hadn't had the opportunity to put it to the test."

Zack reached for the truck door. "Let's test it now." But when he opened it, the outside heat hit him like a wall. He gasped.

"It's probably around 108 degrees by now," Tisha said. She grinned. "Wouldn't you like to take another day to adjust?"

Zack shook his head. "We can't let the killer get that far ahead of us."

Tisha gestured toward Zack's short-sleeved shirt and khaki pants. "Have you got a lightweight, long-sleeved shirt, lighter pants, and hiking shoes hiding in your gear bag?"

Zack nodded.

"Go ahead and get them. You can change in the back of the cab here. I'll set up day packs with water and snack bars. It won't be a walk in the park. Well, not the usual park anyway." She grinned again.

Once Zack had changed, Tisha gave him a pack and slung her own over her shoulder. She wore a sombrero-sized floppy straw hat and handed Zack a straw cowboy hat.

"Two rules of the desert here," she said as they started out. "Always have twice the amount of water you would normally carry on the hottest days anywhere else, and never go without a hat and every inch of skin covered. If you're looking for a nice tan, this is not the place."

Zack glanced at her, curious. "You seem to know a lot about the desert."

"I'll confess," she said. "I grew up in western Nevada, basically just east of here, although strangely, this is my first visit to this park."

Tisha was a strong hiker, and while Zack was no slouch, sweat soon patched under his arms and threatened to run into his eyes. As soon as he wiped his brow with his sleeve, it became dry as a bone. The couloir was very still. The steeply rising ridges above them blocked any breezes. The ancient watercourse they walked in was a mix of sand and small boulders, with fissures in the sand bed surface, reminding Zack of a partially frozen river. He felt like he was in a slow cooker.

Tisha seemed unaffected. If she was sweating, he couldn't tell. She wore light, loose clothing that billowed away from her body.

As foretold, the couloir gradually turned toward the west, and as it did, a slight breeze stirred, a blessing but for the fact that the dry bed grew steeper and the sun was now directly ahead.

Tisha stopped, took water, and told Zack to do the same. "Take a sip whether you want it or not, hold it in your mouth, and swallow it bit by bit."

Although it was not Zack's first time in desert conditions by a long shot, he knew he was in as hostile an environment as he'd ever experienced. He took Tisha's advice without hesitation.

As they hiked, Zack's eyes roamed the couloir for any signs of passage by foot or vehicle. So far, he'd seen none. When they next stopped, he took the opportunity to inspect the ground more closely.

"Anything?" Tisha asked.

"Nothing. Even with the pouring rain in this area, you'd expect a vehicle carrying two people to indent this

47

surface deeply enough to leave an impression, but I see nothing."

Tisha regarded him, hands on hips. "These were not your normal rains," she said. "This watercourse would have been a roaring river. That boulder over there wasn't here before the rains. Out in the valley, they found sections of pavement broken off and chunks of it a half mile away. Badwater Road is still closed beyond our turnoff." She shook her head. "You can't underestimate the power of the flood water."

Zack studied the terrain with new eyes. "Maybe you're right. The event you describe would wipe away even deep tire impressions." He glanced up the slope. "Maybe we can find something when we reach higher ground."

They trudged on. As Tisha had said, the couloir now led west, narrowing and climbing as it did so. After ascending a particularly steep section, they came to a summit. By now, even Tisha was visibly sweating. The slight breeze did not diminish the sun's heat enough to matter. To Zack's mind, their climb of only a few hundred feet seemed to bring them noticeably closer to the blazing orb.

The flat surface of the summit was just fifty feet wide and barren. The couloir fell away behind them, first a narrow rip in the earth, then spreading as it dropped off. A canyon loomed before them. They stood on the south wall, a half mile from the headwall. The ground sloped steeply away, easing as it neared the canyon depth.

"Where are we in terms of the body's location?" Zack asked.

Tisha pointed. "Down to our right is the Second Fall. The First Fall is out of sight around that bend a few hundred feet. The body was found just before the bend. You can see the yellow tape if you look close."

Zack gazed at the slope below them, his eyes roaming its contours to the crime site. He spoke with low intensity.

"Tisha, you might have hit it right on the nose. A body on this steep ground could have tumbled as far as that gentler slope there." He pointed. "Then, if the waters of the flood rose high enough to reach him, they would have swept him down toward that bend in the cliff face. An eddy likely formed there. Once in that eddy, his body would have stayed there." He glanced at Tisha. "Exactly where they found it."

Tisha's eyes followed Zack's pointing arm. She nodded and gave a shiver. "We could be standing on the very spot where the murder took place," she said. Her voice was a whisper.

Zack gave a sympathetic glance. "Seeing this brings it to life, doesn't it?" He looked down at the ground at their feet and scraped it with his foot. It made a sound like sandpaper. "This ground is hard. I don't expect to find any useful evidence, but the scenario makes so much sense that we should use it as a working hypothesis. Do you agree?"

"I do." Tisha took a few steps around the ridge summit, scanning the ground. "Even if the killer had been careless enough to leave a spent cartridge behind, the rains would have washed it away," she said.

"True enough. I don't think there's anything more we can do here. Let's head back to the truck." He gave a sheepish grin. "And the air conditioning."

CHAPTER NINE

"Tippy! It's nice to hear from you again so soon. What can I do for you?" Despite a twisted feeling in his stomach, Simon Barroff's tone was pleasant. It could be the old man was calling to invite him to a social occasion, but it seemed too soon for that. He mentally braced himself.

"Simon, I'll come right to the point. I need to know what happened to that fuel expert."

"Tippy, I told you. We resolved the matter."

"Well, that's not enough. Not anymore. The people I borrowed him from are concerned. They want details."

Simon's stomach did a flip. This conversation was going to be rough. "Do you really think that's a good idea, Tippy? That's Pandora's box. Once it's opened, we all become vulnerable."

Tippy's voice grew harsh. "We're vulnerable now, Simon. These are dark people. They get what they want. You don't say no to these people."

He's *scared*, Simon realized. He began to sweat. "What exactly do they want to know?"

"Where is the body," Tippy said.

"The body? We're talking about heavy ordinance here. What parts of the body do they want?"

Tippy was silent. When he spoke again, it was with quiet intensity. "Forget the cover story, Simon. These men know better. We must tell them exactly what happened to the man, who knows about it, and where the remains are."

"Shit."

"Well?"

"I can't tell you."

"Simon, you still don't get it. We have to give them what they want." His voice dropped even more. "If we don't, Simon, they'll kill us. Both of us."

Simon wiped the sweat from his brow. "You can't be serious, Tippy. I mean, we're public figures, people of rank. To do that—to kill us—would cause a huge furor." Simon gulped. "They—"

"Forget that. How did you get to your position being so damn naive? Accidents can happen to anybody. Especially someone commanding a weapons testing facility, for Christ's sake."

"Shit."

"So just tell me, Simon. Where's the guy's body?"

"I...I don't know."

"Oh, Christ! What do you mean, you don't know?"

"The man I hired to find the guy found where he died but couldn't find the body."

"Okay, who killed the guy?"

"I don't know."

"He wasn't one of yours?"

"No! I didn't have him killed! Why would I?"

"This man you hired. Who was he?"

"He's a Navajo tracker, supposed to be the best."

"Navy Seal?"

Simon gulped. "No, a civilian."

"Wait! You went and hired a civilian to find this guy?"

Simon whispered, "Yes."

There was a prolonged silence.

"Maybe this can work for us," Tippy said at last. "We need to bundle this whole mess onto that civilian. Now listen carefully. Who met with the fuel expert when he arrived?"

"Chief Petty Officer Burk Daly."

"Okay. So the scientist reports to him on arrival, then takes off and drives up the range in a Humvee. Right?"

"Yes."

"So the Chief Petty Officer misses him, grows concerned, and reports the matter to you. You put out the alert, etc.. Okay, so far?"

"That's pretty much what happened."

"Right. Good. That's it."

"That's it? What about the Navajo?"

"You know nothing about any Navajo."

"But I hired him, issued a vehicle to him, and he reported here."

"No, he didn't. No one issued a vehicle or anything else to him. He didn't exist, so how could he report to you? You make sure everyone there is on the same page. You authorized the alert when the fuel expert went missing.

Nothing more." Tippy paused. "Simon, your life depends upon how well you manage this. Do you understand?"

Simon let out a breath. "Yes, Tippy, I do. I'll take care of it." His mind raced. "But the Navajo. People must have seen him. Someone will talk."

"Yes. Someone will talk. People always do. Some civilian comes onto the base waving fake credentials, takes a vehicle, and travels off after the fuel expert. That's what they'll discover. Then they'll look for him. That's it."

Simon's voice was shaky. "Okay."

"Simon, I presume you can control any of your aids who were privy to your meetings with the civilian."

"Yes, I think so."

"You what?'

"Yes, yes, I can."

"See that you do." The phone went dead.

Simon spent the next several minutes shaking like a leaf. He'd never heard Tippy talk like this before, never seen this ugly side of him, heard him sound so *scared*. And now Tippy had dragged him into something that could end his career, even end his *life*.

He thought about the steps he needed to take to disassociate himself from the Navajo. He must remove the connecting links one by one. The first link was Chief Petty Officer Burk Dally. He called him.

=

After leaving the base, Eagle Feather took Route 40 from Barstow to Flagstaff, where he deposited the substantial check he'd received from the Navy at his bank. Then he drove home to his trailer east of Elk Wells, Navajo Nation, and treated himself to a beer and a well-deserved rest. The next day, he had a call from his bank.

"I'm sorry, sir, but your check didn't clear."

"Are you telling me the Navy doesn't have enough money?" Eagle Feather asked.

"No, sir. The bursar who signed the check has refused it, saying he never authorized it. I'm afraid there is nothing we can do, sir. You will need to take it up with him."

After the call, Eagle Feather thought about it. To his mind, there'd been something wrong about the whole operation. He'd uncovered evidence of a professional assassination. And now, it seemed, the Navy wanted to cover it all up and deny him a large amount of money.

Eagle Feather wasn't concerned about the time and effort he'd spent, or even the money, for that matter. The problem had been interesting, forcing him to focus on his tracking skill set. His interpretation of the events written in the sand had been accurate. He'd made his report and closed his mind to anything beyond it. A job was a job.

But this last response by his employers sparked his curiosity. What had changed the base commander's mind? Eagle Feather was sure the order to defund the check must have come from him. He had been the man in charge of the operation.

Now, Eagle Feather let his mind loose to test its analytical skills on the portion of the story he had not explored. Where had the assassin come from, and where had the body gone?

He started with the body. Had the assassin carried the body back to the Humvee and driven it somewhere before returning the vehicle to the motor pool, perhaps depositing it near some ordinance that would disintegrate it?

He thought not. First, doing so would increase his chances of being discovered. A professional assassin would never prolong his association with the body of his victim. Secondly, the tracks returning to the Humvee were not deep enough to suggest that the killer carried extra weight.

To Eagle Feather's mind, that left just one possibility. The body went by air. That meant a helicopter and at least two other accomplices; one to fly the bird, the other to bring the body aboard from the kill site. That solved another mystery in his mind, the question of how the assassin had gotten there. He remembered the two side-by-side toe prints pushed deep into the sand as if pushing off to jump—or an impression left when landing. It must be the latter, probably from the same helicopter.

As his mind churned on, he reviewed the sequence. The victim was given coordinates, possibly by someone at the base, and coerced into driving to them. With clockwork timing, the assassin arrived near the ambush site while the helicopter took itself away to return once the assassin had finished the job. They then flew the body to some unknown destination while the killer returned the Humvee to the motor pool and walked away.

That scenario made sense. The timing was most fortunate for the conspirators because the heavy rains following the murder had erased much of the clues. Eagle Feather doubted other investigators would have found any signs at all.

One thing still bothered him. The footprints left by the assassin, even as minimal as they were, did not suggest the hard edge left by a military boot print. Instead, the edges appeared rounded, as if made by a softer shoe. How could that be? Every military shoe had a sole of some sort, yet the print left by this killer did not. Wouldn't a person returning a vehicle to the motor pool out of uniform seem unusual?

Eagle Feather mentally shrugged. Regardless of that detail, everything pointed to a Navy-endorsed assassination, from the use of the helicopter to the defunding of Eagle Feather's check.

There remained one last nagging question. Why hire Eagle Feather in the first place? Except for the disappearance of the man, something the armed services were always very good at explaining, this very professional killing would have gone unnoticed. So why bring a tracker in to uncover what they had hidden in the first place? And what had later changed the base commander's mind to cause him to cover his tracks all over again?

Then it occurred to Eagle Feather there could be another step in the coverup beyond denying payment: to eliminate the payee.

CHAPTER TEN

By the time Zack and Tisha had returned to Furnace Creek, it was dark. Tisha drove Zack directly to the Death Valley Resort. As bleak and empty as the vastness of Death Valley had felt, seeming to blow dry his soul from his body, the Inn was a miraculous fantasy oasis of stucco and stone, enhanced by towering date palms, exotic plants, and green grass.

Tisha led him to the reception desk and checked into the room reserved for him.

"I'll leave you some time to yourself," she said. "I recommend the Last Kind Words Saloon for your dinner and a beverage." She grinned. "You'll enjoy it."

"Will you be joining me?"

"Sorry, not tonight. I have reports to write." She handed him a card. "This is my mobile number. Let's get together for breakfast and plan our next move. I'll meet you in the dining room. Shall we say seven?" She turned to go, then stopped. "I almost forgot. We have a rental car reserved for you. The desk is holding the key in your name." She gave a wave and walked away.

Zack found his room perhaps more conservative than the hotel exterior suggested but very comfortable, with a pleasant view of palms and green grass.

He unpacked his few belongings, set out a pair of jeans and a collared shirt, and went into the shower. He considered never leaving it, feeling the cool water cascade over his shoulders. When he finally stepped out, he felt chilled in the air conditioning. He knew that as hot as the desert had been by day, it would cool quickly at night, but until then, he would take a beer outside, enjoy the balmy breeze, and think about the case.

He found the Poolside Cafe, decided on a Prickly Pear Margarita instead of the beer, and settled in at a poolside table. The air held a curious scent of desert plants and chlorine, but the drink was delicious.

His phone rang.

"How was the rest of your day?" Janice asked.

"It got better," Zack said. "The ISB agent is very sharp, and we made some progress." He related their theory about how the body arrived where the ranger found it.

"That sounds like a lot of extra time and effort on the part of the killer," Janice said, her voice a question.

"I'm assuming it was a professional hit, based upon the precision shot. In reality, it would probably take less time and effort to hike up the couloir than attempt to persuade the victim to walk the full distance along the Desolation Canyon Trail to the eight-foot fall. Remember, the hit came before the flooding had closed things down. Anyone could have come along that trail at any time."

"Hmmm. I suppose so, although it does seem an exceptional effort by the killer, either way. The victim must have been important to him or whoever hired him. I think the sooner we can identify the dead man, the better."

"Where are we with that?" Zack asked.

"The Park Service ISB shared the DNA of the victim with us, but we found no match in any of our data banks. We distributed his facial photo and description to law enforcement in three states, but nothing yet."

"It's hard to determine motive without an identity."

"Exactly. And Zack, you need to know someone may be attempting to slow your investigation. As you suspected, the blown tire on your airplane was no accident. We found a spent bullet inside it."

Zack took a deep breath. "What kind of bullet was it?'

"There was too little left to identify it precisely, but there is little doubt it was an AP high-density round."

"I think that confirms our sniper hypothesis."

"I agree," Janice said. "And he may not be done with you yet. Be careful." She rang off.

Zack was puzzled. The killer had been very thorough, leaving no trace, no means of identifying the victim, and not even a bullet at the crime site. Why risk it all by shooting out an airplane tire, which accomplished nothing but left actual evidence? Discharging a weapon, even a silenced one, anywhere around a major airport was a huge risk. Why take that chance when the sniper could simply walk away, no one the wiser? Following the same reasoning, why would the killer take even more risks with an attempt to kill Zack, as Janice seemed to imply? It made no sense.

Perhaps the killer was not the accomplished professional Zack had first thought. The attack on the airplane was an audacious mistake, one a true professional would not make. But Zack did not believe the sniper would make another similar one. Having failed in that first attempt, the killer would now disappear. Zack would not be looking over his shoulder.

Night shaded the cut stone facade of the hotel beyond the pool lights into opaqueness, and the decorative lights on the palms brightened as Zack sipped his drink and enjoyed the soft breezes. A few people remained at the pool, the others probably at dinner. There did not appear to be a lot of guests at the hotel due, no doubt, to the many closures in the park.

His mind spun like a caged gerbil on a wheel, thinking about the case. There was so little to go on, so few actions he could take. He supposed he should visit the area in Desolation Canyon where they found the body if only to get the feel of the place. He did not expect to learn much there. He should arrange to get a look at the body, as well. But beyond that, he could only wait for lab results, DNA matchups, and the hope that someone, somewhere, would recognize the victim and come forward.

As his mind went down a checklist, he had a thought and called Janice.

She answered immediately. "Zack, some people go to bed at a reasonable hour."

"Tell me you are not still at the office, and I will sympathize with you."

At her silence, he grinned to himself. "I thought as much."

"What is it?" Janice asked.

"Has someone checked all the security cameras at San Diego International Airport? That sniper made a mistake by shooting at the plane. Maybe it was a bigger mistake than we first thought."

Zack heard a sigh. "Of course. We are reviewing all the footage. We are also interviewing hundreds of airport workers who were present at the time, particularly those in areas not so well covered by the cameras."

"Sorry. I just—"

"And beyond that, we have arranged for satellite footage of the entire airport and the immediate vicinity during the hour before and after the attempt. And, our technicians are studying it foot by foot as we speak."

"Okay, okay, Janice. Just checking."

"Go to bed, Zack. Give your mind a rest. Maybe we will have something for you when you wake up." Janice ended the call, but not before Zack heard a slight chuckle.

Maybe it was the mental suggestion or the consequence of a long day in the heat, but Zack now felt bone tired. He pushed back his chair to stand.

"Buy an old Indian a drink?"

A man in a worn brown poncho and dirty cowboy hat slid into the chair opposite him. One eye squinted out from behind crevices in a face the color of a walnut bowl. The other eye showed white where its lower lid was tugged downward by a scar pulling up at the corner of his lip. The effect was a mirthless, crooked grin. A few rogue hairs sprouted like thistles from his chin.

Zack first wondered how a panhandling old geezer had managed to escape security in this posh resort, but something about the look in his one good eye belied his begging words.

"I know what yer thinking," the old man said.

"If you do, then you know I'm wondering about your brashness in asking for a gift."

"No, you ain't. You're wondering how a cheeky bastard who looks like shit is allowed in a place like this." He cocked up a hip and broke wind.

Zack stood. "I have a long day tomorrow and I'm out of money and patience. Good night."

"Yer just a spoiled Fed who can't find a thief even when he's stealing your pants." He cackled in glee at his own humor.

Zack looked hard at him, then sat back down. "What do you know about it?"

"What about that drink, bozo?"

"That depends upon what you have to tell me."

"I ain't telling you shit until I get my drink."

A distinct unwashed odor wafted toward Zack. He hesitated, then shrugged.

"Okay, what do want."

"A martini, shaken, not stirred." The man cackled again.

"Any particular vodka?" Zack asked, his voice heavy with sarcasm.

"Three measures of Gordon's gin, one of Smirnoff vodka, half a measure of Cocchi Americano liqueur, 'cause they don't got Kina Lillet."

Zack shook his head in amazement. "You think you're James Bond."

"You're not. That's for damn sure."

Zack stood and walked away before the man could utter another insult. He went to the bar and ordered the drink as described.

"Planning to get smashed tonight, are we?" the barkeep asked as he began mixing the drink.

"It's not for me; it's for that old kook over there." Zack nodded toward his table.

The barkeep glanced that way, then grinned. "Oh, him."

"You know him?"

"Oh, yeah." He began rhythmically shaking the drink canister over his shoulder.

"How is someone like that allowed on the premises?" Zack asked.

The bartender laughed and poured the mix into a martini glass. "That's an easy one," he said. "He owns the place."

CHAPTER ELEVEN

When Eagle Feather realized he might have become a security threat to the men who had hired him, he crawled window to window and closed the blinds. His thirty-foot trailer perched on the mesa offered stunning views in every direction but north, where the land rose another hundred feet just beyond a shallow arroyo. The Navajo saw the views as its best feature, and the higher ridge behind the trailer provided reflective warmth from the sun during the winter.

But now, that advantage had become a vulnerability. Agave and sage bunched together like a patched cloak over the red soil, perfect cover for a rifleman. That was where a professional assassin would be—if there was one. From ancestral instincts honed sharp through experience in hunting and being hunted, Eagle Feather acted at even the most improbable possibility of danger.

A small storage shed stood between the trailer and the shallow arroyo marking the ascent to higher ground. That shed was where Eagle Feather stored all his hunting and guiding gear. That was where he needed to go.

He crawled to the far end of the trailer and slithered out the south window where it would protect him from view. He wormed his way along the foundation. He approached the shed by crawling. Once there, he rose to his knees, unlocked the door, and slipped inside.

Eagle Feather knew the ordeal facing him could be a long one. He did not stint on supplies. He selected weapons, ammunition, clothing, and food as quietly as possible, conscious that the thin metal walls of the shed would not protect him from a barrage of bullets.

With his supplies in a backpack, armed with a rifle and knife, Eagle Feather pondered his next move. He put himself in the mind of a professional sniper. The killer knew Eagle Feather was there from his truck parked near the trailer and would wait for his target to appear. A professional like a Navy Seal could wait patiently for hours. But Eagle Feather needed to be gone.

He sat cross-legged and still, studying in his mind the ground surrounding the shed foot by foot. He envisioned three possible avenues of escape, none of them fool-proof.

First, he could try to work his way to his truck and drive away. But there were many flaws in that plan. It was what the sniper would expect him to do, and with it parked on the open ground, it would be almost impossible to reach undetected. He dismissed that idea.

Or, he could worm his way back along the trailer to its rear and crawl down from the mesa with the profile of the trailer between him and the higher ridge. The land sloped steeply and then became a vertical cliff, but once there, he would be out of sight of anyone on the high ground. He thought this was a much better plan and might work, but only if there was one shooter. If a second rifleman waited below, he would be a sitting duck.

His third and last plan was to rush the arroyo. Once in it, he would have decent cover and could follow it most of the way down from the ridge. The arroyo deepened as it fell away and offered good protection so long as the rifleman didn't change position. The third plan was the best, provided he survived the initial rush into the arroyo.

He expected he'd have the element of surprise from his sudden appearance and the unexpected direction of his run; toward the sniper. But the exposure was lengthy, and there was no cover until he reached the arroyo. He needed a way to shorten that distance.

Eagle Feather moved the workbench at the northwest corner away from the wall and, with his bowie knife, pierced the tin wall close to the supporting two-by-four. With a pair of tin snips, he cut a flap just large enough for his body. This hole eliminated twenty feet of exposure. It was the best he could do.

The Navajo strapped the backpack over his chest so it wouldn't snag, crouched before the flap opening, mentally rehearsed his move, gathered himself, and sprang through the hole.

He almost stumbled at first but caught his balance and continued forward. He ran obliquely toward the arroyo, angling west to lessen his profile, even if it did add a yard or two.

Each crouching, running step seemed interminable, expecting with each moment to feel the impact of a bullet. Then the edge of the arroyo was there. The Navajo tumbled down the steep, loose dirt into it. He kipped up to his feet and lunged to the far ravine wall. Protected by that earthen wall, he shrugged off his backpack. He'd not heard a shot during his rush and was beginning to hope his imaginings had all been wrong when he noticed a small hole in the top flap of his backpack.

He knew it was a bullet hole. The bullet had passed through the top flap at an angle, exiting through the side panel, missing his body by a matter of inches. His instincts were correct, and his hunter was an excellent shot. He searched the pack where the bullet had gone and found a ventilated pair of socks. That was the worst of it. Eagle Feather repacked the backpack, slung it on his back, checked the load in his rifle, and moved along the arroyo to the east, opposite the angle of his approach, as a decoy.

But Eagle Feather harbored no more illusions. His ordeal had just begun.

The town of Elk Wells was five miles west as the crow flies but much farther by foot up and down the mesas and gullies that lay in between. The town was the closest source of help and protection. And it was where his opponents would expect him to go. The land to the east was vast and empty, with little water and no cell signals. There was no help that way, so that was the way he must go.

Eagle Feather had no intention of running forever. He had enough supplies to survive several days. He knew the terrain well. His immediate objective was to get off the mesa safely. Then he would assess his options.

As he descended with the arroyo, taking care never to expose himself to view from above, he put himself in the mind of his stalker. Once Eagle Feather had acquired the shelter of the arroyo, the sniper would have a decision to make. A professional would not assume his target would necessarily continue in the same direction he had been moving. The hunter would realize that having lost sight of his armed prey, the tables had turned, and he might well become the hunted. He would have to change position. But where would he go?

Eagle Feather thought he most likely would retain the high ground but must necessarily cast his die and move either east or west, following his best hunch regarding Eagle Feather's choice of direction. If he guessed wrong, Eagle Feather would get away. So, would he expect Eagle Feather to continue, go the other way, or try a double-blind and keep on in the same direction guessing his hunter would expect a reversal? It all came down to a deadly chess match.

The assassin had the advantage of the high ground. On the whole, Eagle Feather thought his hunter would guess correctly and was likely now positioning himself somewhere above him, waiting for Eagle Feather to raise some dust, move a branch, or in some other way reveal himself.

The Navajo knew the arroyo became shallow as the slope steepened and fell away off the mesa. There would be exposure for a distance of some fifty feet. His hunter was undoubtedly training his scope on that very spot, waiting.

Another crux moment in the chess game, he thought. The Navajo could reverse his steps and return along the arroyo and over the ridge where the arroyo remained deep and safe. Unless, of course, he'd guessed wrong, and the hunter was waiting for him there. Eagle Feather didn't like that option, knowing there was too much flat, exposed terrain to cross even if the hunter hadn't anticipated his movements.

So he would go forward. He needed a distraction to make the hunter believe he was elsewhere. He remembered passing a mesquite bush high up on the steep side of the arroyo. He went back to it. He found a heavy, flat stone and took it with him. Once below the mesquite, he removed a T-shirt from his pack and climbed the steep dirt slope to the bush. Selecting a branch of the right thickness and springiness, he bent it down, hung the shirt on the leafy branch, and carefully placed the flat rock on both until its weight, when balanced, held it down.

He had just minutes to return to the exposed fifty feet of the arroyo. Once at its threshold, he set himself like a sprinter on starting blocks and waited. Seconds ticked by, then minutes. He had begun to think his ploy had failed. Then he heard a shot. He sprang across the open area and reached the higher walls of the arroyo beyond.

The springy branch had dislodged from the stone and flung the shirt upward. The sniper had seen it and immediately shot at it. Thus distracted, he'd allowed Eagle Feather enough time to cross the open area.

Eagle Feather one, sniper zero.

But the match was far from over. The killer now knew the Navajo's location, without a doubt. Eagle Feather hurried on, knowing the next confrontation would come soon.

CHAPTER TWELVE

Zack carried the martini and a napkin back to the table and set it ceremoniously in front of the old Indian.

"Forget James Bond," he said. "You think you're Howard Hughes." He resumed his seat.

The old man cackled. "You asked the barkeep a few questions. Good for you." He sipped his drink and made a face. "He's fired."

"You've got your drink. What do you know?"

"I know the dead man was shot at long range by a marksman who knows a thing or two about the weather."

"What about the weather?"

The old Indian's upturned lip pulled into a sneer. "He knew a once-in-a-century storm would bury the victim, you dumb shit."

"Are you always this cordial?"

"Only when I'm talking to a dumb shit."

Zack sighed. "Never mind. How do you know this?"

"My people have lived here for centuries. We know a thing or two about the weather, too."

Zack sighed again. "Not the weather. How do you know about the killer?"

"We keep an eye on the valley."

"Just the good one, I imagine."

The old Indian laughed. "For an uptight fed, you are a funny man." He sipped again, tasting. "Maybe I won't fire him." He rolled his good eye toward Zack. "Ever hear of drones, dumb shit?"

Zack was surprised. Drones. If the man watched over the valley with drones and a drone had flown over the killer...!

"Are you telling me you have footage of the killer?"

"Maybe I do, maybe I don't."

Zack put both palms on the table. "What do you want?"

The old Indian stared back. "Keep the cyanide leaching gold hunting bastards off our traditional lands."

"Are you talking about the Briggs Gold Mine in the Panamint Range?"

"So you do know your ass from your elbow. Yeah, that, the rest of the Range, Conglomerate Mesa, and all the other lands you want to turn into toxic trash heaps."

Zack eyed him calmly. "Personally, I would like to see those lands protected. But as you well know, I'm pretty far down the chain in the government."

"That's the excuse you all use. Man up and take some responsibility."

Zack shrugged. "How?"

"Make a public statement."

"Me? Who'd listen? Besides that, you know FBI agents are discouraged from doing exactly that. When's the last time you heard an FBI agent voice political opinions publicly?"

"That's the point, dumb shit. Because it never happens, people will listen. Do you want my drone footage, or not?"

"There's probably nothing on it I can use, anyway," Zack said, but he felt his defenses crumble.

The old Indian did not answer, just smiled. His teeth were yellow from chewing Pinion nuts.

Zack leaned back in his chair. "Okay, you win. I'll release a statement in the next twenty-four hours. When do I get my footage?"

"After I read the statement and decide I like it."

"I'll write it tonight and send it to you. Do you have an email account, or do you still use smoke signals?"

"Not funny that time, dumb shit. Ask any employee here how to reach me. And by the way, once I get your statement and decide I like it, it is going directly to my media people, so don't think you can pull it back later."

"Never crossed my mind," Zack said.

The old Indian stood and looked toward the bar. "Yeah, maybe I'll keep him another day." Then he walked away.

Zack remained at the table, feeling conflicted. If the old Indian did indeed have drone shots of the killer, even just glimpses from a distance, they would be invaluable to his investigation. He had little else. Even if they managed to identify the victim, they still had a long way to go to find his killer.

Of course, they might get lucky with satellite or security camera footage from the airport where someone had shot at the plane. But again, even if they spotted the rifleman and could eventually identify him, a long shot at best, they had no evidence to link him to the Desolation Canyon shooting.

Every fiber in his being protested against making the public political statement the old Indian demanded. The FBI needed to be seen by the public as apolitical, the servant of the entire nation and all its people, not any particular group or political view.

But his every instinct told him this case was critical, far deeper than it seemed on the surface, a conspiracy he must unveil. He had no doubt the killer was a professional, one of such caliber as to be ranked among the best. That meant a lot of money, the kind of money only big businesses or governments could afford to spend.

One thing he knew—he could not go to Janice for advice this time. Her answer would be unequivocal. Just raising the question would mean losing her respect.

Zack groaned and shook his head. He went to pay his bar bill.

"The barkeep grinned at him "You're all paid up," he said. "You must have had a great conversation with the old guy."

Zack raised an eyebrow. "And you mix a good drink, enough to keep you employed another day."

The barkeep laughed. "I get fired every other day. I'm used to it."

Zack went to his room, reluctant to leave the night breezes and desert smells. Once beyond the pool lights, the display of stars manifested with unusual clarity, somehow reducing the enormity of his concerns to an appropriate size within the universe. But back in his room, his dilemma regrew to feel even more oppressive.

The thing of it was, he agreed with the old Indian. Zack believed in protecting the environment, and calling a halt to cyanide leaching was an excellent place to begin.

He opened his computer and checked the file for news of progress. There was none. No help there. His brain searched endless avenues for answers. He felt like a caged rat.

At last, he returned to his computer and began to type.

CHAPTER THIRTEEN

Chief Petty Officer Burk Dally read and re-read the memo concerning the death of Chief Petty Officer Second Class Dash Holiday. He remembered the man by name because it brought to mind a strange combination of the killer Doc Holiday and Christmas. Wasn't Dasher one of Santa's reindeer? He might even have seen the guy once or twice at the motor pool where he worked. The man died from carbon monoxide poisoning due to improper ventilation in a garage where he was working on a transporter late at night.

Dally grunted to himself. It must have been a rush job to keep him at it into the wee hours, some high brass wanting the vehicle fixed yesterday. Improper ventilation? That seemed like a novice mistake. He shrugged and scrolled past the memo to the next item. Every death on his watch upset him, but he knew by now not to dwell on it.

It wasn't as if Dally didn't have his own problems. Ever since his assignment to escort that civilian tracker, that Navajo, around the base, things had become weird. He was sure someone was watching him. He'd seen the same guy several times now in different places. It was usual to see faces he didn't recognize from time to time as he went about his business—after all, it was a huge base. But this guy kept turning up everywhere and never seemed to be doing much. The next time he saw him, he planned to demand his name, rank, and serial number.

He remembered the look on the base CO's face when Dally offered to check the flight logs for a possible overflight of the range where the scientist had disappeared and how the CO told him in no uncertain terms to stand down. Leave it alone, in other words. Soon after that, the CO's aide came to him and whispered that it would be better if he forgot the whole business.

The following memo in his computer was the technical fuel expansion tolerance analysis for a specific set of circumstances he had requested, but his mind drifted back to Holiday. He'd seen something else with this guy's name on it not long ago. What was it? Then he remembered. His name was in the vehicle pool log book Dally had read when searching for the missing scientist. Holiday had issued the Humvee to the fuel expert.

Dally inhaled deeply. Shit! Suddenly, Holiday's careless mistake took on a more worrying significance. Was his death more than an accident? Could someone be running around eliminating all connections to that missing fuel expert? Killing witnesses?

Then Dally chuckled. Come on, now! He watched too many spy movies on TV. Accidents happened all the time on the base.

=

At Command, Command Chief Simon Barroff was reading the same memo, but he had no illusions about the significance of the words scrolling down his screen. He reached for his phone and enabled a secure line. He punched in a number, let it ring nine times, and hung up.

Five minutes later, his phone rang.

"What's going on, Simon?"

"I called to ask you that very question, Tippy. What's going on?"

"Please explain."

"Tippy, I won't tolerate this. I've got a dead motor pool mechanic, coincidentally the same one who signed out the Humvee to your fuel expert. I told you I'd guarantee the silence of my people, that I'd handle it. Now you've—"

"Hang on, Simon." Tippy's words cut through like a razor. "I've done nothing. But I told you these people are deadly serious and demand absolute security. They don't agree with your assessment of who can be trusted."

"Tippy, I won't tolerate this! I demand you call them off, or—"

"Or what? What will you do, Simon? Think before you answer that. Would you report it? To whom? What if you reported it to the wrong person?"

Simon went silent, chagrined. How deep did this conspiracy go?

"Listen, Simon, we are old friends, and I'd hate to see something happen to you. Don't think for a moment your rank and position will protect you from these people. If they heard what you are saying, they'd kill you. I can protect you just so far and no more. There was an unfortunate accident on your base. It happens. Live with it."

The line went dead.

Simon Barroff felt his control ebbing away. This whole matter had gotten way out of hand. Was there no place he could turn?

If this was a conspiracy involving even one of the upper brass, Simon dared not report it.

Where would it all end? Others had seen this man Sweiger during his short time on the base and had interacted with him before his disappearance. Were they all destined to die?

Simon clenched his jaw as anger grew in him. This base was his command. He'd achieved it through rigorous and disciplined attention to duty. He had earned his reputation as a strong leader who cared for his people. He was damned if he would curl up in a ball under his desk and allow it to happen, to see his command undermined, his reputation shattered. Someone on this base was a murderer who did not belong here or was a traitor. Maybe he couldn't kick this can upstairs without endangering his life, but he could make it difficult for the murderer who was now within his domain.

He reached for the phone to call in his aid, then changed his mind. These orders needed to come from him directly. He turned to his computer.

11 June 22

MEMORANDUM

From: Command Chief China Lake Naval Air Weapons Station

To: All Base Personnel

Via: Command Chief

Executive Officer

Subj. IMMEDIATE BASE RESTRICTIONS

1. All personnel are denied leave effective immediately until further notice.

2. All base visitors (including consultants, spouses, and family of base personnel, and all personnel assigned to this station within the last fortnight) are to be restricted by their executive officer and held under observation until further notice.

3. This base is shut down. No one may enter or leave, including base personnel returning from leave, or navy personnel of any rank, unless personally approved by the Command Chief until further notice.

S. N. Barroff

Command Chief, USNR

Copy to:

Base Website

Simon had no illusions about the uproar he would cause as he punched return. But if people were planning to commit murder on his base, he would not make it easy for them.

CHAPTER FOURTEEN

Eagle Feather stopped in his tracks. He had come to the juncture of his narrow, ancillary arroyo with the larger arroyo at right angles to his path. Before him, a butte rose vertically four hundred feet, its exposed sandstone face glowing in the afternoon sun. Now he must make another move in his chess match: turn left or right. It was a simple decision but one with game-ending implications. Left meant going higher, to climb alongside the mesa he'd just descended, closer to the sniper. But if undetected, he could obtain higher ground and turn the tables. Turning right was the safer choice but the one most likely to be anticipated by his opponent.

But something else caused Eagle Feather to freeze like a startled deer. A footprint was in the sand before him, clear and sharp as if etched in clay, dust along its edges unmoved by wind or moisture, left within the hour by someone wearing a moccasin. No other prints were near it. There was just the solitary footprint.

Someone had placed the footprint deliberately. It was a message, and the news was not good. It told Eagle Feather more than one person was hunting him. It told him someone had anticipated his escape route. It told him his next decision was likely a matter of life or death.

The toe of the print pointed toward the uphill side, but Eagle Feather did not see that as an accurate indication as the wearer had deliberately placed it. Had the wearer expected him to assume a direction from the print and go the opposite way, or was it, again, a double-blind?

He could not wait and deliberate. He kept in the cover of the uphill wall of the intersecting canyon and moved up it, using all his skill. By moving toward the first sniper, he hoped to bring his two pursuers closer together. Or, the second assassin might wait for him in the opposite direction. If not, he would be somewhere above him up this arroyo. In any case, he should be safe from an attack from behind.

The arroyo narrowed and deepened. The sun baked within the earthen trough, but near the shaded wall was some relief from the heat. He stepped carefully, knowing a single dislodged pebble could give him away.

As he climbed, he thought about his hunters. He had assumed they must be Navy Seals or members of some highly trained group of Navy men, but the moccasin print raised new doubts.

Who would wear moccasins for an assassination? Not the military, at least not any force he knew. He must be facing hired killers. That made sense, now that he thought about it. The Navy could not risk being identified with this killing if things went wrong.

But why the footprint message? Was it a taunt? An attempt to intimidate him? Or a design to trick him?

The moccasin print message said, "I know what you will do before you decide to do it." The killer was saying he could read his mind. And so far, he'd been right. It was not a comfortable thought.

Eagle Feather went over his plans. If he had guessed right, the first rifleman would now be moving along the mesa summit ridge toward a place overlooking the headwall of this arroyo where he could set up his shot and wait for the Navajo to appear.

The second killer should be ahead of him somewhere up this arroyo. Eagle Feather had seen no sign he'd passed within this gully and concluded he must be climbing outside somewhere along its rim.

He thought about the topography the killers must traverse and, guessing how long it would take them, the Navajo concluded they should both be beyond his position, one nearer his gully and one higher on the mesa ridge, each focusing on the terrain near the arroyo headwall and the upper arroyo itself. Now was the time to make his move.

Eagle Feather climbed the ten feet of steep dirt of the uphill wall of the arroyo by kicking steps in the soft soil. Peering over the top, he surveyed the mesa slope for several minutes, listening and watching for movement. There was none. He squirmed over the edge and into a sage thicket. After another minute of listening, he began his crawl directly toward the mesa summit, hoping in his mind to create a hypotenuse to a triangle defined by the two points that were the locations of his adversaries.

It was a move so risky no one should suspect it, so exposed that discovery meant death. It was the right move.

The Navajo crept on despite his discomfort with utmost care and patience, blending like a shadow. But if he took too long, his hunters might wonder where he was and change their positions. He could not allow that.

He was not far from the apex of his climb when he knew he had succeeded. He heard a cough off to his right, a bit downhill, exactly where he expected the first rifleman to be.

He crept on until he found enough cover to rise to his knees and peer out. He saw dense growth in the area of the cough. He waited. A minute later, he saw sage branches move.

He settled into position for his shot. His target shifted his weight, revealing he was kneeling, his rifle trained down the slope. The man had assumed an uncomfortable body position and moved to rest various body parts. He was an easy target.

But Eagle Feather needed to find the second killer. If he shot now, that assassin would move and remain dangerous. So the Navajo waited, his eyes flicking between his known target and downslope toward the arroyo.

The second hunter was also patient. Eagle Feather had begun to despair of finding him. Then his near target spoke aloud, startling the Navajo. He was talking into a radio.

Eagle Feather heard the voice emit from a second radio farther down the slope. His eyes went there, and he saw an object sail into the air from the mouth of the arroyo. It was a radio. The second killer had tried to dispose of it before it could reveal his location. But it was too late.

The Navajo aimed his rifle there and fired. Without waiting to see the result, he swung his rifle and shot twice at the first killer, then returned his aim downslope and fired twice more. He searched the area with his scope. There was no movement.

After several minutes, he guessed the man was dead or seriously wounded. Still cautious, he moved silently to the position of the near killer. He saw a boot, then a leg in camouflage pants. He moved in and found a large man dressed in a hunting outfit sprawled before him. A Steyr SSG 69 sniper rifle was tucked beneath the body.

The rifle told him little, as he knew it to be a popular weapon worldwide, but he knew it was a professional sniper's weapon of choice. His two shots had penetrated the man's temple and throat.

He kept his attention tuned to the second rifleman's position while he searched the body but found nothing. There were no labels on his clothing. Eagle Feather was not surprised. He took a picture with his phone, then left the body as he had found it.

Now he began to work down the slope toward the second killer. There had been no movement at this location that he could detect during the five or eight minutes he'd spent with the first man's body. If alive, this other man could have escaped or moved to a second position to ambush Eagle Feather as he approached. With that in mind, the Navajo circled wide, staying to cover, studying every bit of sage and brush bunch, ready to react instantly.

He approached from below. The sniper had chosen a group of agave plants for his concealment, their thick blue-green leaves forming a tunnel over the bare dirt between them. It would have been impossible to discover a man in camouflage tucked in among the needle-sharp leaves. The impatience of his partner had been his undoing.

But the man was gone.

Eagle Feather crouched and studied the dirt beneath the agave. It was clean, wiped by an expert hand.

It meant that while Eagle Feather examined the body of the first sniper, this man was wiping away evidence of his presence so carefully that the Navajo had seen no movement, even while watching for it. Had he been less cautious in his approach, he might have died. He still might be in peril.

He spotted a blotch of red on the underpart of an agave leaf. Lower on the plant, he saw several smaller drops of blood and a broken leaf. One of his shots had grazed the man. A small flesh wound, no doubt, but maybe enough to cause the killer to retire from the field.

If so, he would likely have retreated to the arroyo and used it to escape. If not, well, the man might be anywhere.

Eagle Feather did not linger. He wormed out of the agave stand and crawled down the slope toward the arroyo. Only within its high banks could he feel some measure of safety.

He slid down the soft earth side and into its shelter. The sun was lower now, the arroyo entirely in shade and cooler. Sweat and grime covered every inch of the Navajo's body. He could not return to his trailer, which meant a long, chilly hike to the nearest safe location. More misery awaited him, but he was alive, and one of the killers was dead.

As he rose from his crouch, his eye went to a line in the dirt. He looked closer. It was another moccasin print.

CHAPTER FIFTEEN

"I met with an aged Native American today whose manner belied his good heart and concern for his tribe. He descends from a people who celebrate the earth and its bounties and live simply from its gifts, replenishing what they take and living in balance with nature. Disastrous flooding this past year swept over the land, scarring it forever and greatly diminishing the people's resources. The great rains were from nature but not by nature. The scars on the land were from flooding but not natural flooding. All of it is from acts of men, not nature. Man is the butterfly whose flapping wings on one side of the planet affect the entire world. Our acts: our industrialization, our pollution, our stripping of the land of its forests, and our poisoning of the land with toxins have inevitably led to the destruction of the land where this old Indian dwells. Once, our acts were from ignorance, but now they are acts of stubbornness, greed, and denial. Because now we know better."

Zack paused his typing and took a deep breath. He had set out to write a simple homily and ended up writing a sermon. Zack shook his head. If he released a statement like this, it would certainly not end well for him.

He read over it. What could he remove? As a man of honor, how could he dilute the truth on the page before him? He could not.

Was it worth his career, his stable universe, to publish this statement to obtain some film footage that might or might not help him solve this case?

But was that the real issue? Had he agreed to make a statement just because the old Indian had leveraged him?

Zack knew the answer. And he knew the old Indian knew the answer. It was not about the case but about something more. It was about his own core belief to value, preserve and protect. And the old bastard had known it.

Zack sighed. There was no point in putting off his decision. He knew what he must do. He punched send.

That night Zack tossed and turned despite the comfortable bed and air-conditioned room. He vacillated between regret and resolve in his mind. Was it better to be true to himself or protect his position, livelihood, wife, and son?

Despite Zack's many years as a valued FBI agent and administrator, he knew the agency's unofficial rulebook consisted of one rule: never embarrass the FBI. By some people's standards, he had just done that.

He felt Libby would be okay with his statement; she would likely applaud it. So would his son, although financing his continuing college would become an issue without Zack's pay. Yes, they would muddle through somehow. But Zack loved his job and respected his colleagues. He would hate to go out this way.

Zack punched his pillow and rolled to his side. This damn tape better be worth it, he thought. Even if they fired him before he could finish the case, Tisha, the ISB agent, might be able to resolve it, provided the film footage was detailed enough.

Zack rolled over again and thought about the old Indian. What a clever bastard! He'd played Zack like a piano, likely studied his profile, and knew exactly how to approach him to get what he wanted even before Zack arrived. No wonder the old guy owned a resort!

Zack was up by four a.m., unable to sleep longer. He made coffee with the in-room pod machine, read his messages, and glanced at the news as he sipped his coffee. At five a.m., there was an email with an attachment. It was from owner@deathvalleyresort.com.

Zack sighed and read the message.

"You write well for a government lackey. Congratulations, you passed my test. I will not publish your words under your name (unless your real name is anonymous). I'd rather keep you on the case. The drone footage is attached."

Zack let out a long sigh of relief. He'd just spent a long, restless night worrying for nothing. But no matter. He had the footage and the respect of the old Indian. The best of both worlds, he thought. He moved the cursor to the attachment and opened it.

It took several minutes for Zack to comprehend what he saw in the film. The picture was high resolution, but a dark cloud cover cast the terrain with a grey hue, muting the vivid colors of the sandstone striations. He had no sense of location from the film until he was hurtled headlong into a confining space with walls rising on either side. He realized they were flying up a canyon. Was it Desolation Canyon? They whipped around tight bends at great speed. It nearly nauseated him. He saw what he thought were flashes of a trail beneath and maybe one of the falls. From the occasional glimpses of the canyon depths, he guessed they were flying at an altitude of a hundred feet or so, just under the canyon rim. After rounding a particularly tight bend, Zack spotted movement on the right side of the picture, almost level with their flight elevation. The drone operator saw it too, for his view suddenly turned to the canyon wall, searching, then settling on a tiny running figure leaping and sliding down it. Rain had begun to fall, and its curtain blurred the figure when at that moment, it stopped and turned to look back up the slope, threw its arms wide, and fell backward as if propelled. It landed on its back with limbs spread wide and lay still. The drone moved closer to the downed figure. It became distinguishable as a human, entirely naked. A wave of rain beat down and obscured the figure for a moment, but not before Zack saw diluted blood flow from the man's head.

The drone turned its camera up the slope where the man had looked, rose higher, and searched along that line of sight. It showed a ridgeline and flew above it to scan it. A figure came into the frame. The operator held on to it. The figure was slinging a rifle over its shoulder. It wore a hooded garment and a small backpack.

Zack paused the image, sat back in his chair, and breathed out. Here was the killer. The drone was fifty to eighty feet above, more or less, and the rain was heavier now. The camera filmed the figure through a gray haze. The killer was slender, his loose clothing billowing in the wind. Zack could see no more detail than that.

He released the pause button. The figure was moving away, down the far side of the canyon wall. The person's movement, even seen through the hazy mist, was smooth and graceful, as that of an athlete striding efficiently. Then the figure became obscured by a gusting downpour of great intensity. The drone pilot moved closer. The figure came back into view. Without hesitation, he unslung the rifle from his shoulder and turned it on the drone. A flash of intense light came from the barrel. The drone pitched wildly, and water pooled on the camera lens as it oscillated between sky and ground. Then it steadied, and the earth fell away below with great speed. The footage ended.

Zack shook his head, incredulous. The sudden, swift movement of the rifle from the figure's shoulder to such a precision shot was startling. Scary, in fact. It was like watching someone shoot skeet while standing backward, aiming by sound rather than sight, and hitting the target. And all that in a high wind and heavy rain.

It was incredible that the drone operator had been able to regain control. The killer must have thought he'd demolished the drone. Yet there must be some concern in his mind. Might the camera be recovered, or had the footage live? What would he do, Zack wondered. A professional assassin would try to find out if tape existed, and there was no doubt in Zack's mind this was an elite professional.

He imagined the killer would go online to determine who would or could fly a drone in the teeth of a storm up Desolation Canyon; and why. He might assume the park service flew it to check that no one was in the canyon with the storm coming on. He'd research everything available about the park personnel and safety strategies, but he'd come up empty. He'd never suspect a wily old Indian.

Zack slapped his leg in glee. This drone footage was poor luck for the killer and good luck for Zack. He restarted the clip from the beginning and settled in to analyze it, image by image.

CHAPTER SIXTEEN

His momentary joy at his good luck turned to pensiveness as Zack studied the film repeatedly, noting the extraordinary capabilities demonstrated by the killer. Not only had he planned an almost perfect execution by removing all clothing and means of identification from his victim, but the killer had managed to utilize a once-in-a-century weather event to help hide the body. It was bad luck that someone had found the body at all. By the odds, it should have remained buried forever.

Then, the power and reflexes of the individual evidenced in the film were exceptional. Here was a formidable opponent.

Zack sobered as he realized other than a bit of film showing how the death had occurred, he had nothing else. He could not identify the killer and was no closer to identifying the victim. He could not even determine the weapon used because of the poor quality imagery due to the storm.

So what had he learned? He read over his notes on the hotel notepad.

He knew he was dealing with an elite professional killer, probably internationally known. He would contact Interpol and ask who among the assassins they regularly attempted to locate might have been in California on that particular date.

He knew such an assassin came at a high price, sustainable only by the extremely wealthy, a country, or a global business. Therefore, the victim must be a man of consequence to one of the above. It was unlikely the victim was local. He might even be from another country. They would need to expand their DNA and facial features search beyond national borders. They needed to search the world for news of any missing man of consequence.

The assassin was an exceptional marksman, possibly holding records and awards from armed services or gun clubs at the very least. This person practiced regularly and probably utilized a range somewhere habitually.

Zack sighed. He knew very little. But he did seem to be having some luck, and hopefully, the bad luck would continue for the killer.

His phone buzzed on the table. It was Eagle Feather.

"White Man, I need you to process a body."

"Eagle Feather! Where are you?"

"In a motel somewhere."

Zack waited, but the Navajo did not elaborate.

"Okay, so where is the body?"

"Up on the mesa ridge behind my trailer."

"Last I knew, you hired on to find a missing person somewhere in the desert. Is this the missing person?"

"No, White Man, this is someone who did not want me to find the missing person."

Zack caught up mentally. "So he came looking for you."

The Navajo's silence was his answer.

"Why not just tip off the Navajo Nation Police? Let Jimmy Chaparral deal with it."

"It is not a local matter. It would come to your people anyway. Are we going to play twenty questions now?"

"No, no. I'll report it to Janice. Why aren't you home?"

"White Man, we must talk. Where are you?"

Zack told him. The Navajo ended the call without another word.

Zack knew Eagle Feather would find him in his own good time and resumed thinking about his case. But before he could focus, there was a knock on his door.

He opened it to Tisha Knolls, her eyes bright, exuding energy. "Are you ready for breakfast?"

Zack took her arm and brought her into the room. "Before we eat, you need to see something."

"Uh, okay." She allowed Zack to steer her to a seat at the desk.

Zack started the film. "Watch it through and give me your thoughts afterward," he said.

Tisha's face had a puzzled expression as the movie began, then she gasped as she recognized the surroundings. When it ended, she leaned back and stared at him.

"Where did you get this?"

"I'm not at liberty to tell you at the moment, but suffice it to say this film is genuine."

"Can we look at it again, slower?'

Zack replayed it. They paused and studied several images, exchanging comments on what they saw.

"Well!" Tisha said. "Now we know what we're up against."

Zack did not tell Tisha about the nagging foreboding in his mind.

They went down to the dining room for breakfast. It was seven a.m., and service had just begun. Zack was not surprised to notice the old Indian sitting alone at a table near the window. If Billy had seen them, he gave no sign of recognition.

Zack wondered what the old Indian thought about the drone footage. Probably a lot more than he let on, Zack guessed.

"What's next?" Tisha asked, sipping her coffee.

Zack cocked his head. "I was hoping for your thoughts."

Her return gaze was speculative. "You were absolutely right about the killer and his method. Almost as if you were in his mind."

Zack shrugged. "I simply thought about how I'd do it myself."

"Have you dealt with many professional killers?"

"Just one or two."

She stared at him, then looked away. "Well, to answer your question, I'd involve Interpol. A killer like that must have a reputation."

"Agreed."

"But we have no real description to offer."

"Also true."

"But I suspect an assassin this good takes the whole matter to another level. Beyond my pay grade, for sure."

Zack grinned. "You're not getting out of it that easily. You and I are stuck with this, no matter where it leads, partner."

Tisha stared into her coffee cup. "This man, this victim, must be pretty important to somebody."

Zack nodded.

"I wonder what the killer did with the victim's clothing?"

That startled Zack. He hadn't thought about it. "Maybe he burned it. How does that matter?"

"It might not. But why not leave his clothing on? I mean, why not just empty his pockets and remove his clothing labels? How could his clothing make that much of a difference?"

"We can do a lot with clothing fibers, microscopic bits of soil, even DNA," Zack said. "I'd love to have had some clothing for our lab to work on.'

Tisha shook her head. "It just seems to me the killer went to an excessive amount of trouble to hide the identity of his victim."

They ate in silence for a while.

"Was the killer a man or a woman, do you think?" Tish asked suddenly.

Zack thought about it. "Well, I assumed a man, but the fact is, it could be either. The drone film shows nothing to help us in that regard, just that the killer is an elite professional. That is all we have to work with."

He put down his fork. "I'm going to contact my boss and get access to files on all internationally known assassins, including those of Interpol, CIA, M6, and others. I hope to end with a list of top-level assassins who could have been in the area."

He paused as a thought came to him. "There's something I should have told you." He went on to tell her about the sniper at the airport. "We can't be sure it was the same sniper, but it was a helluva shot."

Tisha frowned. "Of course, it's got to be him. That's too much of a coincidence."

"My thinking as well."

"It means, if true, this killer knew you would be the one investigating and wanted to delay you." She paused. "But what would that accomplish, do you think?"

"I've been asking myself the same thing," Zack said. "Why would a short delay in my arrival time here matter? In fact, why didn't the killer simply take me out? He had plenty of opportunity."

"They'd just replace you, and the uproar following the assassination of an FBI agent would be enormous." Tisha looked thoughtful. "Maybe it was a warning shot, a 'keep away' message."

Zack stood. "Maybe. But if so, it failed. I'm going to my room to call Janice. What are your plans?"

"I'm going back to the rim of Desolation Canyon to see if I can locate the exact spot where the drone filmed the assassin."

Zack was puzzled. "What would that accomplish? The rains will have wiped away all traces. We saw that yesterday."

"Just a hunch," Tisha said and smiled. "

CHAPTER SEVENTEEN

After Tisha departed, having insisted on billing the meal to her expense account, Zack went to his room and called Janice, who picked up immediately.

"Our mutual Navajo friend tells me there is a body on the high ridge behind his trailer," Zack said.

"Hmmm. He just stumbled across it, I suppose. Did he happen to have anything to do with it?"

"Most likely, although he was ambiguous. He seemed to think the situation would end in our laps sooner or later."

"Where is Eagle Feather? I want to talk to him."

"He's gone to ground. He wants to meet with me. I expect I can tell you more later."

Janice sighed. "Okay, I'll send an agent to find the body and establish jurisdiction. Call me when you know what the hell is going on."

"Thank you. On another subject, we have proof positive that we are dealing with an elite assassin here. I want to know who among the known professional killers could be in the U.S. in this time frame."

"I have some resources at Interpol," Janice said. "I'll take care of that. You think he's still around?"

"I suspect he may be keeping an eye on our progress. The airport incident was not a coincidence."

"You think the killer learned you were coming to investigate the case and tried to stop you by shooting an airplane." Janice sounded dubious.

"I think it was more of a shot fired across my bow," Zack said.

"That would be most unusual for an assassin of this caliber." Janice paused. "Unless, of course, there is personal history between you."

There it was, the elephant in the room, the thought— the dread—that had been in the dark recesses of his mind all along.

"Maria," he muttered. "I think I've been sublimating that possibility."

"Well, don't. I also think it's time to go global with the DNA of the victim as well. The entire matter could have originated half a world away."

"Have you had any luck with the airport camera searches?"

"Nothing. We were able to narrow down some possible sniper positions from angles to the aircraft wheel at the time, but that left a huge area uncovered by cameras."

"What if...." Zack hesitated. "This killer responsible for the Desolation Canyon shooting showed extraordinary planning. If he is also the airplane shooter, he somehow knew I'd be flying from that airport in advance and even knew the exact flight I would be on."

"How is that possible?"

"Why did the taco truck owner suddenly change his mind and file suit against me? Why did the judge demand an immediate deposition? It feels like the whole side trip to San Diego was bogus. Was that a coincidence as well?"

"You think the assassin knew about the taco truck incident, forced the owner to complain, and pressured the judge in some way to order an immediate deposition just to get you to San Diego and then on that particular flight the next morning? Why?"

"I think he wanted to keep me out of it."

"Zack, that would be a lot of effort and risk just to keep you away. And that is exactly what Maria would do."

This time the silence was longer. Janice broke into it in her usual brusque manner.

"I don't have to tell you to be careful."

"No, you don't."

"We'll pursue this case like any other with no assumptions. I will do all I can to learn the killer's identity. I'll speak with the taco truck owner and the judge. If they verify our suspicions, we will go from there. Otherwise, we have nothing but guesswork."

"And gut feelings."

"And gut feelings."

"By the way, Janice, I have a short film to send you. It is drone footage of the killing. The images are unclear, nor did we learn much from them except to prove the killer is a professional assassin. I hope your lab people can get more from it."

"Actual footage of the killing? You might have mentioned that at the beginning of our conversation. Yes, send it. We'll see what we can learn."

Once the call ended, Zack pushed send, and the film went on its way. But his thoughts were on Maria.

There was a knock on his door.

Zack took his handgun from the drawer.

"Who is it?"

"Open up, White Man."

Eagle Feather stood at the door. He looked exhausted. The Navajo looked warily around the room.

Zack moved the hand with the pistol from behind his back and put the gun in the drawer.

Eagle Feather raised his brow. "Expecting company?"

"Just a precaution. I'll explain. You look like hell. How about a cup of coffee, first?"

"Thank you."

Zack put the pod in the machine and poured in water, glancing at the Navajo. "Janice is handling your problem, but she wants answers."

"It is simple," Eagle Feather said. "The navy changed its mind and decided to kill me instead of pay me."

Zack turned from the coffee maker and stared at his friend. "What happened?"

"It's a long story."

"I've got time."

Eagle Feather sat in a chair and described the discovery of the ambush site and his conclusions. "I gave my report to the commanding officer, and they cut a check. But later, they changed their minds and decided not to pay me. They even went a step beyond and sent two killers. I got one of them, but the other got away."

Zack gave an involuntary grunt. "We may be at opposite ends of the same case. You have a missing body, and we have an unidentified corpse with a hole in his head."

"Here's the part you won't like, White Man," Eagle Feather said. "The killer that got away was Maria."

"But she always works alone," Zack said.

"I thought that until I found her moccasin print. It was a deliberate message. It was Maria."

A knock at the door startled them.

"Are you expecting anyone?" Eagle Feather asked.

Zack shook his head. He took the handgun from the drawer and held it behind his back.

Eagle Feather slid his knife from his belt, moved to the side of the door, then nodded.

"Who is it?" Zack asked.

A muffled female voice responded. "It's Tisha."

"Are you alone?"

"Well, yes, of course."

"Where were you raised, Tisha?"

There was a pause. "What's going on, Zack? I told you, I was raised in Nevada, just across the border."

Zack smiled and nodded to Eagle Feather. "It's okay."

CHAPTER EIGHTEEN

Zack took Tisha by the arm and, after a glance both ways down the corridor, ushered her into the room, slipping the safety chain back into place.

"What's the big deal, Zack? I just came by to see if we could meet for lunch today to compare notes—Oh, hello. Who is this?"

Eagle Feather stepped from behind the door and, sheathing his knife, walked back to his chair.

"I'm glad you stopped by, Tisha," Zack said. "Our plans have changed. You are not going back to the kill site."

Her blue eyes rounded. "I'm not?"

"Come. Sit down. I'll explain."

Zack motioned her to his vacated seat at the desk and went to perch on the edge of the bed.

"First, let me introduce my long-time friend and associate, Eagle Feather."

The Navajo nodded.

Tisha put out a hand. "I'm Tisha Knolls from the Park Service Investigative Services Branch," she said, her eyes curious.

"Tisha has been working closely with me," Zack said. He turned to Tisha. "But now we need to change our procedure."

"Okay."

Zack paused, thinking about how to explain things.

"We believe we know the identity of the killer. Maria is an assassin of the highest caliber. She gets top dollar. Whoever hired her has deep pockets."

"How do you know who she is?"

"She told us," Zack said. He gestured toward Eagle Feather. "Or rather, she told him."

Tisha shook her head, bewildered.

"You better start at the beginning, White Man," Eagle Feather suggested.

"You're right." Zack sighed. He pointed between himself and the Navajo. "We have dealt with her twice before. The first time, she escaped. The second time, we caught her, but only after she nearly killed Eagle Feather." He glanced at the Navajo. "Then, she escaped while being transported from prison to court for her trial. Next thing we knew, she was in Morocco."

"But how does he know our killer is this Maria?" Trisha asked.

"Eagle Feather was hired to investigate the disappearance of a chemical engineer from the China Lake Naval Air Weapons Station."

"Right next door."

"That's right. He found an ambush site but not a body. After reporting his findings and returning home, he found his large check had bounced. The Navy denied ever issuing it. Right then, he began to suspect a conspiracy and realized whoever was behind it might consider him a loose end. My silent friend here never wastes time on emotion. He assumed he was under threat, and he was right. Two shooters ambushed him and he managed to kill one of them. The other escaped but not before leaving a signature footprint for Eagle Feather to see, one he knew well."

"You think his sniper and our killer are the same person?"

"Yes, I do. It all fits."

Tisha was silent, thinking.

"I know it's a lot to process," Zack said. "But if our killer is Maria, and I believe she is, we must approach this investigation differently. We must always assume we are targets. Meaning, you are not to go to Desolation Canyon on your own."

Tisha's blue eyes flashed. "I can look out for myself."

Eagle Feather spoke for the first time. "We thought so, too. We were wrong." He turned to Zack. "I may have winged her, but not enough to slow her down. I do not believe she knows I came here."

"If she is our killer, she will come here anyway," Zack pointed out. He scratched his head. "Let's see if the chronology fits for her to abduct your scientist, bring him here to kill him, attack my airplane, and still get to Arizona in time to ambush you."

The two men compared days and times.

Zack did the math. "The time is tight," he said. "But for her it is doable."

"You two make her sound like some kind of phenom," Tisha said.

"She is," Zack said. He turned to Eagle Feather. "I have a film I'd like you to watch."

He arranged his computer so they all could see the screen and played the drone footage. As it progressed, they paused it from time to time, studying the slim form of the assassin.

Eagle Feather grunted. "That is Maria," he said.

"How does this change things?" Tisha asked.

"With Maria, it's a personal matter. She likes to play games. Deadly games. But only within the scope of her contract. Her business always comes first."

Tisha looked from Zack to Eagle Feather. "What was she contracted to do?"

"Probably to eliminate that fuel expert, for whatever reason," Zack said.

"So she has completed her contract."

"She will kill anyone she believes is a witness," Eagle Feather said.

"She'd be gone by now, except for Eagle Feather," Zack said. "She would believe he has figured out the truth."

"Where is she now, do you think?"

Zack glanced at Eagle Feather. "She is here. She knows we work together. She also knows that together we can figure out the whole story."

"But her cover is blown now. Wouldn't she leave?"

"She would not leave knowing that Eagle Feather can connect the missing scientist from China Lake to the body in Desolation Canyon. He is the only credible witness who can bridge that gap," Zack said. "Besides, I told you she likes to play games, especially with Eagle Feather. And I do not doubt if the opportunity arose to take out the three of us, she'd seize it."

Tisha thought about it, seeming much chastened. "But she'd have no reason to assassinate me unless I am with you and Eagle Feather. Right?"

"I would not bet my life on that," Eagle Feather said.

Zack nodded. "It is not safe to make assumptions regarding Maria."

"Still," Tisha said, rising, "I'm the least likely target of the three of us."

Zack looked at her with concern. "What do you have in mind?"

"What I started to do this morning," she said with a stubborn look. "To go back to Desolation Canyon and search for evidence. I know from seeing the film exactly where she was at the time."

"What could you possibly expect to find?"

"I doubt she stopped to search for the shell casing after shooting the drone. I might be able to find it. That would add to a chain of evidence."

"You do not understand," Eagle Feather said. "She picks up her shell casings. A storm would not stop her."

Tisha looked from one man to the other, frustration showing on her features. "What do you two plan to do, then? Hide?"

"In a way," Zack said. "There is more to Maria than we have told you. First, you should know she is a he, or he is a she, dependent upon her needs."

"A transvestite!"

"Or transgender, perhaps, but not from an inner need to be one or the other gender, more of a fluidity of gender. Maria changes to blend into the background, like a chameleon."

"You always refer to her in the feminine."

"That was her identity when we first met her." Zack felt a wave of emotion with the memory.

"And she is Chemehuevi," Eagle Feather said.

"She is Native American?" Tisha's eyes rounded in amazement.

"Yes," Zack said. "I believe she will come here to finish her work. When we look at this vast expanse of desert surrounding us, it might appear there is nowhere for her to conceal herself. But what better place to hide than among those who share her indigenous cultural heritage, like a pebble in gravel."

"The Timbisha!"

Zack nodded.

Tisha was beginning to grasp the situation. "They own this resort. She could be anyone here - a waiter, housekeeper, security, anything!"

"Room service?" Zack added.

"My God! If what you say is true, we are trapped here."

"I'm glad to see you begin to share our paranoia," Zack said, with a grin. "It is better to be cautious than careless where this person is concerned. However, it's not quite as bad as all that." He glanced at Eagle Feather. "We have some time before she can insert herself into the staff."

Eagle Feather shook his head. "If she is here now, she will move quickly."

CHAPTER NINETEEN

When Eagle Feather's phone rang, it startled him. He usually kept it muted when he carried it at all, which was seldom. He grunted and accepted the call.

"Is this Eagle Feather, the Navajo tracker?"

"Yes."

"As you may recall, we spoke in my office at the—"

"I remember."

"Yes, enough small talk. We need to meet."

"Why?"

"Certain information has come to my attention that affects you. I think it's in both our interests to meet."

"I have no reason to trust you."

"I understand. Therefore, we should meet at a place of your choosing. But soon."

"Call me back in one hour." Eagle Feather put his phone away and glanced at the others.

"That was the base commander at the China Lake Navy facility. He wants to meet."

Zack's eyes narrowed. "Why?"

"I do not know."

"Do you think he is compromised?"

"It is hard to say. My report seemed to surprise the commander at the time."

"This could be a trap," Tisha said.

Eagle Feather shrugged.

Zack watched Eagle Feather's face. "Do you think you should meet?"

"If he is not compromised and wants to meet, that could only be to try to find out more about the abduction. That would be good," Eagle Feather said.

"On the other hand, if he is compromised and wants to meet, that could mean he wants to eliminate you where his hired assassins failed," Zack said.

"What will you do?" Tisha asked him.

"I will meet him."

Zack nodded. "Let's get some help with this." He turned to his computer to send a message. A moment later, he had a reply. Ten minutes later, there was a knock at the door.

"Who is it?" Zack called.

"Little Bo-f***ing Peep."

Zack grinned and went to the door.

The old Indian stood framed there. Zack waved him in. The others stood when he entered.

The Timbisha glanced at Tisha, then stared at Eagle Feather.

He looked to Zack. "You registered as a single guest, dummy."

113

Zack grinned and turned to the others. "Let me introduce my new acquaintance and the owner of this resort, Billy Frank."

They all stared at each other. It was indeed a strange gathering.

The old Indian looked at Zack. "Time is money. My money. What do you want?"

"We need your help to find the killer," Zack said. "The assassin is likely here right now, somewhere in this resort."

"You want the shooter from the drone footage, and you think he is here."

Zack nodded. 'We know who the assassin is but need your help to find her."

"Her?"

Eagle Feather spoke. "She is a Two Spirit person. She was born Chemehuevi."

Billy studied Eagle Feather. "You are Navajo," he said.

Eagle Feather nodded.

"How do you know this about her, Navajo?"

"We have hunted her before."

"And failed."

"Yes," Zack said. "That is why we need your help."

"I would expect a fed to fail, but not a Navajo." He turned to Tisha and contemplated her. "Did you fail too?"

Tisha drew herself to her full height. "I have not yet tried."

"Umm." He turned to Zack. "If you find this killer among my staff, there will be a shooting. People will die."

Zack nodded. "That is why we need to draw her out where no one can be hurt."

"You have a plan."

"Yes. But first, we need to tell you what we know."

Zack brewed more coffee while the three told their part of the story. It was the first time they had exchanged such a detailed report. There was a flurry of questions and answers. During it all, the old Indian listened but did not speak.

"It is complicated," the old man said at the end. "What do you want from me?"

"You know this land. We need a place for Eagle Feather to meet Commander Barroff in an isolated place, but one we can cover with hidden rifles. He would likely approach by helicopter. We must protect Eagle Feather should the commander come in a gunship."

"Anything else? Would you like a Dairy Queen nearby?"

"Yes, please," Eagle Feather said.

The old Timbisha sat unmoving, thinking. Then he said, "Why should I involve myself and my people in your problem? Go and meet with this Navy man somewhere else. Then maybe the killer will follow you away from here."

"There is nowhere else uninhabited enough to isolate this combustible situation from the general population," Zack said.

"We have authority to act here within the National Park," Tisha added.

"The assassin is here. Your people are already involved," Zack said.

Billy stood and shuffled to the door. He turned to Zack. "I have helped you once, as we agreed. You must help yourself now." He waved an arm. "Badwater Salt Flats covers two hundred square miles. Even you should have no problem finding a private place." He walked out.

"Well! Some help he was!" Tisha said.

Zack shrugged. "At the least, he is warned and can take steps to safeguard his staff and his people. But we still need a place for Eagle Feather to meet the commander."

"We have it," Eagle Feather said. "He just gave it to us."

Tisha turned to him in astonishment. "Badwater Salt Flats? Have you been there? It is flat as a pancake and white as snow. There is no place we could hide out there."

"You are right," Eagle Feather said. "It is white as snow. White on white disappears when viewed from the air."

Zack caught on. "Camouflage! Like that used by the 10th Mountain Division. We can hide in plain sight." He turned to Tisha. "You know the area. We need a coordinate for a place we can reach on foot but is far enough away to discourage tourists and park personnel."

116

He glanced at Eagle Feather. "When the commander calls, you can give him the coordinates and arrange to meet tomorrow morning, say at 0800 hours when the sun is low in the east, and we can arrange to have it behind us. That will allow a day for my boss to find camo for us." He glanced at Tisha. "Can you use a sniper rifle?"

"Oh, yes!"

"Excellent."

"When you call Janice, ask her for several cans of that fake snow, the kind you can spray onto your Christmas tree," Eagle Feather said.

Tisha and Zack looked at the Navajo in astonishment.

He explained. "When we walk on the salt lake surface, our feet will leave footprints that he will see from the air. The prints will lead right to where we are. We must cover them as we walk, or our camo won't help us."

Zack stared at his friend, whose inventive mind always surprised him.

"Fake snow it is," he said.

117

CHAPTER TWENTY

"How will we find this mysterious assassin?" Tisha asked. Before she kills us, preferably," she added.

Eagle Feather settled the meeting details with Commander Barroff during a return call, who accepted the specifics they proposed. Now the talk had turned to more immediate concerns.

"I believe old Billy Frank had the answer to the first part of your question," Zack said. "When we move out tomorrow for the meeting with Barroff, she will certainly follow us. We must plan for that."

Eagle Feather gave a dismissing grunt. "Do you think she will ever do what we expect?"

"Of course not. Maria never does," Zack said. "But we'd be foolish not to plan for it anyway."

"There is another matter," Eagle Feather said. "When she came for me at the trailer, she had company. Someone might be with her now."

Zack nodded. "Do you think Maria knows you are here?"

"She may have guessed it. She knew our two cases were connected, even if I did not. But I know she did not follow me."

"Good. Let's keep it that way. You stay in this room until the meeting tomorrow." He turned to Tisha. "We will carry on as before over the next several hours. You and I should go to lunch as you had intended." He glanced at

Eagle Feather. "Get some rest, my friend. I'll bring some food back for you. Meanwhile, no room service, no maid service, no reason for any hotel personnel to enter this room."

"I could use the sleep," the Navajo admitted.

Once they heard the safety chain engage on the closed door behind them, Zack and Tisha walked to the elevator.

"What can you tell me about the Timbisha Shoshone," he asked Tisha while they waited. "Maria could be hiding among them. Besides, I'd like to figure out what makes that old Indian tick."

"I don't know a lot about them," Tisha said. "But I do know someone who can tell us."

Lunch was a nervous affair for Zack. Every guest, every waiter, every person they encountered became Maria in some clever disguise in his mind. After finishing their sandwiches, they brought food back for Eagle Feather, then walked to Tisha's pickup truck.

"Where are we going?" Zack asked.

'We're going to the Indian Village," Tisha said. "It's where we ate that first day. The village is an unincorporated Timbisha Shoshone community." She grinned at Zack. "It's a hundred and ninety-seven feet below sea level and hotter than hell.

"That's nothing new around here," Zack muttered.

"About fifty tribal members live here now. When the National Park Service finally gave up trying to move the Timbisha people out of the park, the Civilian Conservation Corps built housing for them. That was in 1938."

119

"How do they live?"

"Not very well, on the whole. As a tourist attraction, largely. Billy Frank owns the resort, and some other members run the restaurant. They sell souvenirs and crafts. They've been trying to construct a casino project on some other tribal land, but it's hit a snag."

They drove past a welcome sign and entered the village, a collection of boxlike adobe and stucco buildings tucked among trees and desert growth.

Tisha pulled to the side of the road next to a house built in part with adobe bricks and the remainder of stucco. As she opened the truck door, an older woman wearing round, tinted glasses, a simple blouse, and slacks appeared on the porch and watched them. Zack felt a stillness and serenity about her even at that distance.

"Thank you for agreeing to see us, Mrs. Flores," Tisha said, extending her hand.

Tisha turned to Zack. "You are in the presence of a celebrity," she said. "Esther has single-handedly brought worldwide recognition to her people and their conservation concerns."

Esther's age-lined face creased into a fleeting frown. "Not the world, not yet, anyway," she said. She looked at Zack. "You are the FBI man."

Zack nodded. "Zack Tolliver. I'm honored to meet you, ma'am."

She gave his finger the slightest touch for a handshake and beckoned them toward the door. "It is cooler inside."

Zack stepped around a dusty bicycle and followed the women inside the house. The thick walls held the coolness from the previous night well. It was pleasant.

They were in an all-purpose room with a mix of brightly colored carpets covering the entire floor, a desk overflowing with papers against the far wall, and a TV on a small table nearby. There was a worn couch and two overstuffed armchairs. Sunlight issued into the room from a deep casement window.

"Sit," Esther said. "I will bring some tea."

Zack perched next to Tisha on the couch. He sent a curious glance around the room. Stacks of books were on the floor next to the desk and in various clumps against the wall here and there.

Esther reappeared with two cups nestled on saucers. A sage and cinnamon scent drifted to his nose.

"You are looking at my book filing system," Esther said. "The piles may appear careless, but each is arranged topically for quick reference. The stacks change with each project." She handed them their tea and seated herself in a chair. "The topic du jour is arsenic leaching."

"A mining procedure," Zack said.

Esther nodded. "Arsenic kills the land as surely as it kills people."

"The Alset Corporation mine?"

"Among others. To the men who want to extract the minerals, the Panamint Hills present an opportunity. They know and care little for the spirit of the land and its connection to all creatures."

121

"I recently spoke to another who holds your views," Zack said.

Esther smiled. "My brother, Billy."

Zack raised his brow.

"I see your surprise," she said. "People seldom guess we are siblings. We look and behave differently, but our hearts are united. We fight for our land and our people."

"Your land?"

Esther waved an all-encompassing hand. "My people have lived in this land for thousands of years, ever since the Ancient Ones inhabited the earth. The land always provided our needs, and we lived from it in harmony with all creatures." She settled her gaze on Zack. "But you are here for another reason."

CHAPTER TWENTY ONE

"I'll cut right to the chase," Zack said. "There is a dangerous assassin hiding in Death Valley. This killer has already struck once. We believe she will strike again. We think she may be hiding among your people."

Esther nodded, her lined and weathered face remaining calm. "I know about the man murdered in Desolation Canyon. I have spoken with my brother. Why do you think this killer is still here?"

"I have met this killer before. She will not leave loose ends."

Esther's eyebrow had risen at the word 'she'. "What loose ends?"

"That would be me," Zack said.

"If you go away, the killer will go away?"

"It's not that simple," Zack said. "Your brother may have become a loose end because he has knowledge that could hurt her."

"The drone footage."

It was Zack's turn to raise an eyebrow. "You know about that."

"As I have said, my brother and I are of one heart and mind."

"So you understand how important it is for us to locate her."

Esther's gaze went to some distant place. "We are a small community," she said. "As in many small communities, everyone here knows everyone else's business. We survive because we have each other." She turned her gaze back to Zack. "I have not heard of strangers in our midst."

Zack gave her a business card. "If you should learn about a stranger, any stranger, it is important for you to contact me."

Esther took the card. "Why has this killer come here to kill a stranger?"

"That is a good question. I do not have an answer."

Tisha glanced at Zack and spoke to Esther. "It may be because of the isolation here. She was unlucky. By all odds, her victim's body would have remained buried deep under the mud flow. She was also unlucky that the drone flew up the canyon just when it did."

"But so much trouble to bring someone here to kill them. That is hard to understand," Esther said.

Zack grimaced. "There is very little we understand about this assassin."

"What do you know about the victim?"

Zack shrugged. "Very little. He was a scientist, apparently, who consulted with the Navy before she killed him."

Esther's eyes flashed. "The China Lake Naval Station?"

"Yes." Zack eyed her curiously. "How did you guess?"

"The Naval Station is our neighbor. The land they took for their weapons testing is the land of my people. We are no longer allowed to go to those places important to our culture." She raised her brows. "How was this man kidnapped from a military installation that is so protected?"

"He had taken a vehicle and driven down the weapons range for some reason. It was there, far away from the facility, that the assassin intercepted him."

"Ah. Perhaps the scientist was searching for the caves."

Zack and Tish glanced at one another.

"What caves?" Tisha asked.

Esther smiled. "There are many myths and legends about caves in the Panamint Mountains. Those mountains have always been a place of mystery from the earliest time of my people. The name, Panamint, originates from the Paiute word Panümünt or Pa, for 'water' and nïwïnsti for 'person'. Do you wish to hear more?"

"Yes, of course," Zack said.

Esther put down her cup. "I will tell you first about the Kingdom of Shin-au-av, which means God's Land. Far back in time, an important Paiute chief lost his beloved daughter. His grief was great, and he felt he could not live without her, so he decided to follow the trail of Indian spirits to the land of the dead. He entered the cave and traveled deep into the earth, beset by many dangers, until he came to the glorious sunshine and green land of Shin-au-av. A beautiful maiden met him there and led him to a great room where countless happy dead Paiute danced. The chief despaired at finding his daughter among so

125

many, but he followed the maiden's advice and sat to watch the people pass and waited for a glimpse of his daughter. At last, he saw her, and they reunited in joy and love, and the chief took his daughter's hand to lead her home."

Esther paused, extending the dramatic moment. "Before they departed, however, the beautiful maiden warned the chief not to look back on his journey home. They ran from that place, hand in hand, but the chief could not resist one last backward glance at the place of such beauty and happiness. At that moment, he found himself alone. He returned to his people, a saddened man, but brought with him the news of the wonderful kingdom of their destiny, Shin-au-av."

Tisha's eye's glistened at the telling of the story. "That is so romantic...and sad."

"It reminds me of the story of Lot's wife from the Bible," Zack said.

Esther nodded. "The story of Sodom and Gomorrah. Lot's wife looked back and turned into a pillar of salt."

"Was the cave passage to Shin-au-av supposed to be in Death Valley?" Zack asked.

"No, but nearby, in the Panamint Mountains region. But I can tell you another story of an underground kingdom, not from Paiute legend this time, but reported in white men's newspaper accounts."

"Please do," Zack said.

"The first record of it comes from a prospector named White, who claimed to have fallen through the floor of an abandoned mine into an underground tunnel. Following it, he came to a room where hundreds of human mummies lay surrounded by treasures. He said there were many other tunnels, which he did not follow."

"Where was this?" Zack asked.

"It was reported at Wingate Pass in the Panamint Mountains. Of course, few believed the tale, and when someone volunteered to accompany White back into the tunnel, he could not locate it again."

"That's it?" Tisha asked.

"That should have been it," Esther said with a smile, "but about twenty years later, there was another newspaper article about a man who located a tunnel in the same region which led to burial chambers for giants, people over eight feet tall, as well as a ritual hall of ancient people with walls carved with hieroglyphics. He claimed to have found thirty-two caves covering a hundred and eighty square-mile area."

Zack gave a smile of deep skepticism.

Esther smiled back. "Yes, these tales are similar to many legends and tales of lost treasures and lonely prospectors. But in fact, the Wingate Pass area has produced many minerals that are sought after by men, including gold, now mined with cyanide leaching even as we speak. What is to say my ancient forebears didn't possess such treasures?"

CHAPTER TWENTY-TWO

"What do you make of the cave legends?" Tisha asked Zack. She accelerated along the gravel road, a dust cloud rising behind them. The air conditioning worked mightily to dissipate the heat built up while the truck sat in the sun.

"It does add an interesting element to this case," Zack said. "I'd like to know how close the abduction site was to Wingate Pass. Why was he headed to that area?"

"Let's look at a topo map," Tisha said.

"Okay. We can use my computer in my room. We'll need Eagle Feather to confirm the abduction location."

Zack's phone sounded with the particular call sound he used for Janice. He picked it up.

"Any luck with the camo?" he asked.

"We have it," Janice said. "And we found the snow spray cans as well. I'll leave it to you to explain that particular expenditure to the accountants."

"That's great!" Zack said. "How will you get it to us?"

"A UPS truck will deliver it all to the ranger office at Furnace Creek addressed to agent Knolls at 5 p.m. this evening. The carton will have a National Park Service return address."

"Perfect," Zack said. "Have you learned anything about the fuel consultant abducted from the China Lake facility?"

"Hmm. When you told me about that possible connection, I looked for an investigation by the Navy or by any other federal organization, but I found nothing. No one reported the disappearance. In fact, there is no report of the man arriving on base. It's as if he never existed, whoever he was. Zack, it feels like we are going against some powerful forces here."

"No DNA matches for the victim yet?"

"Nothing. Any scientist who is an expert in propellent fuels should have an educational and experiential background in the field that we can trace. But all the data lists have come up empty."

Zack thought about it. "Maybe he was not what he pretended to be. Maybe he was not there to consult about fuels at all."

"What else could he have been there for that demanded such secrecy?" Her voice grew edgy. "We can't get a handle on this without knowing anything about the man. And the Navy isn't helping."

Tisha glanced at Zack as he put down his phone.

"Anything new?" she asked.

He shook his head. "Nothing. No DNA match for the victim. It's like trying to find a ghost."

Back at the resort, Eagle Feather was awake and let them into the room. He had enough rest and listened closely to their report of the conversation with Esther Flores.

"What do you think about those cave legends?" Zack asked the Navajo.

"I would not think much if not for the Paiute story. White men will lie for their own ends, but Indian history passed down from ancient times is oral, not written, and tends to be accurate. Native American legends are likely to be based on fact."

Tisha's eyes sparkled. "Do you think there might be caves with treasures in the Panamint mountains?"

Eagle Feather looked amused at her enthusiasm. "I would not discount it." He turned to Zack. "Any luck with the camo?"

"All set. It is being shipped to Tisha at the ranger station, along with the fake snow, scheduled to arrive at five today."

Zack glanced at Tisha. "We'll check some topo maps. I'd like to see the abducted site related to Wingate Pass and Desolation Canyon."

Zack opened his laptop. With Tisha and Eagle Feather peering over his shoulders, he brought up a topo of southwestern Death Valley. He widened it to include the Naval Air Weapons base.

Eagle Feather placed a finger on the screen. "That is where the scientist had gone. He left his vehicle there and walked here."

Zack zoomed the satellite image. It showed low sand hills. He placed a marker on the map.

"Now to find Wingate Pass." He put the name in the search bar, and it appeared. Then he zoomed out until both markers fit on the screen.

"It's a long way," Tisha said. She sounded disappointed.

"With a mountain range in between," Eagle Feather added.

Zack studied the screen. "Not so far as the crow flies," he said. "If he expected to be picked up by an aircraft from there, it would be a short trip."

Eagle Feather grunted. "I saw no signs of aircraft."

Zack peered at him. "Yet the man had disappeared. And if he is the same man Maria killed at Desolation Canyon, he had to come even farther."

"It is a problem," Eagle Feather said.

"As we have said in the past: if the only solution left to us is the impossible, then the impossible is the only solution. "

"Meaning?" Eagle Feather asked.

"Meaning somehow there was a way to transport the victim. We don't know how yet, so we must defer the answer and move forward with two assumptions. First, the victim expected to be transported to his objective since we know there was nothing at the place where he disappeared. Second, the abductor knew about the transport and used it to her own advantage to bring her victim to Desolation Canyon."

Zack raised questioning eyebrows at Eagle Feather and Tisha.

Both nodded their agreement.

"So where does that leave us?" Tisha asked.

"With a trip to find those caves," Zack said.

CHAPTER TWENTY-THREE

"Why the caves?" Tisha asked. "We don't know if they even exist."

Zack shrugged. "I know it's a long shot, but we have nothing else. This scientist, this fuel expert, went to a lot of trouble to reach a barren, remote spot in the middle of nowhere. He must have had a destination in mind. Then he disappears. I'm guessing he expected to have transport somewhere. The only place of interest in the direction he was driving is the Wingate Pass area." Zack shrugged. "It's a long shot, but we won't know until we go there and look around."

"First things first," Eagle Feather said. "My meeting with Commander Barroff could change things."

"That's true," Zack said. "Let's prepare for that." He entered the GPS coordinate for the meeting into the topo map search engine, and a marker appeared. Zooming in, they found themselves staring at an expansive patchwork quilt of salt, white amoeba-shapes with thin dark outlines.

"Our camo will be perfect for this background," Zack said.

"And it will be difficult for Maria to follow us closely without being seen," Eagle Feather said. "The nearest cover is miles away."

"I think we can assume that Commander Barroff will also be checking out this GPS position," Trisha said.

"He should like it. It couldn't be more isolated," Zack said.

"Will he land if he doesn't see anyone there?"

"I will be there," Eagle Feather said. "He will see me."

"No," Zack said. He gave his head a shake. "If he has hostile intent, you'd be too easy a target. You need to hide and wait until he lands."

"Then he might not land, and we'll never know his intentions."

Tisha held up a hand. "Wouldn't he circle the area to scout it?"

"Probably."

"Then he would see our vehicle and assume Eagle Feather is inside it. He would land, expecting Eagle Feather would then come from the vehicle."

"She's right," Zack said, turning to Eagle Feather. "You should stay hidden until the bird has landed. Once he is down, we can cover you."

Eagle Feather shrugged. "Whatever you say."

The large carton arrived from UPS later that afternoon. Zack and Tisha spent the next hour sorting and fitting the camo, assembling sniper rifles, and sighting them in. They organized ammo and two cans of fake snow into camo pockets and then went to dinner. They made their final plans in Zack's room that evening.

In the morning as the sun peeked over the eastern hills, they piled into Tisha's truck and drove to Badwater Salt Flats. Their gear was in the truck bed, and Eagle Feather was in the cab, hidden behind tinted windows. The red, rising sun began its daylong searing of the flatlands below.

By the time they drove past the entrance to Desolation Canyon, the temperature outside the truck had climbed to over eighty degrees. There had been no sign of any other vehicle on the road.

Zack kept an eye on the GPS coordinates on his phone as they drove along. They arrived with an hour and a half to spare.

"Let's suit up," Zack said.

"It will be bloody hot lying in those suits out there for an hour," Tisha said. "Are you sure?"

"We can't take a chance on Barroff arriving early and spotting us walking out there," Zack said. "Or Maria coming along, for that matter. We'd be sitting ducks."

She reluctantly agreed.

As it turned out, it was slow and meticulous work to spray over their footprints as they walked. They diverged as each moved toward their agreed-upon positions.

Once he reached his assigned place, Zack stretched out in a prone firing position, sighting toward the expected landing place of the aircraft. After checking that his suit covered him from head to toe, he settled in to wait. He was wet with sweat in short order.

He dared not move, even to check his watch. The camo suit was intended for use in snow and cold, not in a desert, and had no ventilation. The heat grew like a furnace. Zack had a water bladder with a hydration hose. It was his only relief. The wait seemed interminable.

Zack gained some small satisfaction glancing at Eagle Feather's position. The Navajo was invisible. The camo idea was working.

Sweat would be a problem sighting through the scope, Zack realized. He was contemplating wiping his eye when he heard the distant thwack-thwack of an approaching helicopter. The craft hovered above the designated landing zone for several minutes, then lowered into his view in a flurry of blowing salt.

Once the wheels touched, the pilot cut the engine, and the props slowed, allowing the dust to settle. Zack faced an open hatch door where a 50-caliber machine gun pointed directly at him. Then the pilot door opened, and a tall man in battle fatigues climbed down from the helicopter to the desert floor. He walked several yards toward Zack, then stood still. His body filled Zack's eyepiece.

With an authoritative gesture, the man pointed his finger directly at Zack and motioned for him to come to him.

At that moment, Eagle Feather rose from the salt near Barroff like a ghost.

The commander spoke to him, then pointed to Zack again. Eagle Feather waved Zack forward.

As he arrived, two ice blue eyes under bushy brows fixed on Zack, who felt like a student called to the teacher's desk. Then the eyes turned to Eagle Feather.

"You have every reason not to trust me. I understand that," the commander said. He spoke softly, but his voice had authoritative clarity.

"You sent an assassin to kill me," Eagle Feather said.

"I did not, but I'll address that in a moment," Barroff said. "First, call in your henchman before someone makes a mistake." The commander nodded toward the 50-caliber gun.

Zack tried to bluff. "What henchmen?"

"A prone rifleman is at my eleven at three hundred yards. He must be very uncomfortable. You are amateurs playing a professional game. The camo is good, but you didn't plan on infrared. Your heat signatures were clear as day from the air. If I wanted to harm you, you would already be dead."

Zack hung his head. He should have thought about infrared.

Barroff gave a tight smile. "And don't forget the one in your vehicle. I need to know he's not a threat."

Zack looked up, startled. "In the vehicle?" It came clear to him in a moment. "Get down!" he yelled.

He heard the sound of an impact on metal. Immediately, the fifty-caliber opened up with a tremendous roar. Zack lay flattened on the baked salt earth, watching parts fly from the distant truck. It erupted in flames.

"Jesus!" he muttered.

Barroff was already back on his feet and running to the helicopter. "Get your people aboard," he yelled.

Zack hollered at Trisha, standing, staring at her truck. She turned and began to run toward them.

The big gun stopped firing. The silence was deafening.

"Get in the helicopter," Zack yelled. He lay down protective fire toward the burning vehicle.

Tisha reached him, breathing hard from running, her face etched with shock.

"Get aboard," Zack yelled. He stood and retreated behind her, walking backward and firing from the hip. Eagle Feather began firing from the helicopter. Zack turned and dove through the open hatch as the bird lifted off.

Eagle Feather kept shooting until they were airborne. The gunner motioned them into safety belts attached to the hull. The helicopter veered and raced toward the smoking truck hulk, keeping the gunner aligned to the target.

From the forward seat, the commander gestured for Zack to put on earphones.

"Who was that?"

"The assassin," Zack said.

The helicopter angled steeply toward the flaming truck and circled it.

"He's dead now," the commander said.

But Zack knew better. "No. Keep searching."

The bird kept circling.

"No one could have survived that," the gunner yelled.

Eagle Feather leaned toward him. "Look for tracks leading away from there," he yelled back.

"There are no tracks," the gunner said.

"Zack spoke into his mic. "Commander, make wider sweeps around the truck. She must be here somewhere."

The commander spoke to the pilot, and the helicopter edged farther out. Barroff turned his head to Zack. "She?"

"You have no idea," Zack said.

CHAPTER TWENTY-FOUR

The helicopter widened its radius around the burning vehicle while everyone aboard scanned for signs of life. They saw none.

"It's time to give this up," Barroff said. "No one could have survived that."

"Can your infrared detect a body in that truck?" Zack asked.

"No chance. The heat of the fire is too great."

"Then we need to land and see for ourselves."

"Not happening. There may be other snipers at this location. I'll not risk the ship." Barroff instructed the pilot, and the bird lifted and leveled into direct flight.

"Where are we going?"

"To find another place to land where we can talk."

Zack settled back against the bulkhead, feeling frustrated. He exchanged a dark glance with Eagle Feather. They knew Maria had a habit of managing miraculous escapes.

They flew for ten minutes before the helicopter hovered and descended into another expanse of desert, near low hills tufted with green brush and the lavender Panamint Mountains beyond.

The engine noise stopped, the props whipped and slowed above them, and Commander Barroff climbed from his seat and came aft to join them.

"We can talk here," he said. "There are no roads or dwellings near here."

The commander rounded on Eagle Feather, his intense gaze boring into him. "Who just tried to kill me?"

"I think she was trying to kill all of us," Zack said.

Eagle Feather returned Barroff's gaze. "How do we know we can trust you?"

Barroff stared at the three of them. "Okay, I'll give you some background." He hesitated. "I know Eagle Feather, but who are you two?"

"I'm Zack Tolliver with the FBI." He brought his card from beneath his camo suit and passed it to Barroff.

"I'm Tisha Knolls with the Investigative Services Branch of the National Park Service. I don't have my card, but these men can verify my identity."

Barroff grunted. "How the hell did you two get involved? All of this is Top Secret." He turned a suspicious eye on Eagle Feather.

The Navajo remained calm. "Two assassins tried to kill me and nearly succeeded. I think you need to convince me you did not send them."

"That's acceptable."

Barroff sat on a bulkhead bench and spread his hands. "Someone in Navy Command sent a man reputed to be a top expert in propellent fuels to the base without notifying me. I first learned of this when my aide reported him missing. A short time later, an old Navy friend called to say he had sent the expert to us. When I told him the man had

141

disappeared, he became threatening. I hired Eagle Feather to track the consultant at my friend's urging because civilians are not required to file reports. Later, when I reported his findings to my friend, he insisted the entire affair remain secret as if it had never happened. He is my superior officer with powerful Washington connections, so I agreed, but I wasn't happy. I hoped that would be an end to it. But when men under my command who had been in contact with this civilian had fatal accidents, I drew the line."

Barroff's face turned to granite. "I closed down the base, no one in or out. We detained and interviewed every unauthorized person on the base and searched every nook and cranny. We found nothing." He turned to Eagle Feather. "I asked to meet with you because I hoped you would have some clues to these killings."

"I think we do," Zack said. "I was brought in to investigate a body discovered by park rangers in Death Valley. We found actual drone photos of the killing. When Eagle Feather arrived, we learned two assassins attempted to kill him. He killed one, and the other escaped, but we think we know her identity, and I believe the cases are connected."

"You think your victim might be my civilian?"

"We hoped you could answer that question," Zack said. He reached beneath into his camo pocket. "I have a photo on my phone."

Barroff studied the photo and returned the phone to Zack. "I never saw him, and I don't recognize this man," he said. "But send the photo to me, and I'll show it to someone who did see him."

"We believe the same assassin has come here to eliminate loose ends," Zack said. "I think we can assume our victim is your scientist and move forward with that assumption."

"It seems likely," Barroff said. "Maybe we can confirm that with your photo." He glanced at Eagle Feather. "What happened to the body of the assassin you killed?"

"The FBI has it," Eagle Feather said.

Zack affirmed with a nod. "We will attempt to identify him, but I doubt we will succeed. Elite assassins don't leave a trace."

Barroff's eyes held Zack's. "Then how do you know the identity of the killer who just shot at us? The drone footage?'

"No, the images were unclear, but her methods are familiar."

"She left a signature sign, so I would know her," Eagle Feather added.

"She?" he asked again.

"It's a long story," Zack said with a sigh.

"Okay, I'll take your word for it."

"Who is this man who sent the civilian to your base?" Tisha asked.

"He is an old colleague," Barroff said. "But I believe he is under the influence of someone else. He is scared. He won't talk."

"Maybe it's time for you to come in from the cold and enlist our help," Zack said. "I know just the person to handle this."

"The FBI?"

"Yes. "

Barroff sighed. "I can't tell you how much I hate this situation, and yes. I need help. But I don't know how far and wide this conspiracy ranges or who I can trust."

"You can trust Janice, my boss," Zack said.

"I must trust you and your colleagues at this moment. But the people behind this will not hesitate to harm me or anyone associated with me in this case."

Zack felt sympathy for this man who had so much to lose. "Janice has never let me down, even when her career has been on the line. She won't let you down."

Barroff nodded. "Okay, have her reach out to me. What will you do next?"

Zack glanced at Eagle Feather and Tisha. "We will try to discover where this supposed fuel expert was trying to go."

CHAPTER TWENTY-FIVE

The helicopter touched down on the small airstrip at Furnace Creek just long enough for its passengers to disembark and flew off again as soon as they were clear.

They stood alone on the fiery runway in white camouflage like three Ghostbusters, holding their scoped rifles.

Tisha made a call. "They're sending a ranger to pick us up," she said after she finished. "This camo may be hard to explain," she said, glancing down at her attire. "But if I remove it, I'll be left in my undies."

Zack grinned. "Best not try to explain. Leave them wondering."

"I've got another call I have to make," Tisha said, her expression grave. "Please excuse me, gentlemen." She walked a short distance away with her phone.

The airstrip radiated heat beneath Zack's feet like hot coals. He slipped out of the sleeves of his camo suit, letting it drop to the waist, but it didn't help much. "I hope they get here soon," he said.

"Did you know we are standing on the lowest airstrip in North America?" Eagle Feather said.

Zack raised a sweaty eyebrow. "Well, you certainly are the random facts dispenser."

Eagle Feather shrugged.

Tisha strode back to them. She pointed to an approaching vehicle. "There's our ride."

Minutes later, they climbed into the air-conditioned truck. The frigid air in the chilled cab was almost too much after the heat they had experienced.

"Now I'm too cold," Zack said.

"White people are never satisfied," Eagle Feather said.

Tisha's phone sounded with a segment from Chopin's Funeral March. "It's my boss," she said, answering. They heard her say, "Yes, ma'am," many times before she ended the call.

"You're in trouble for losing the truck, I bet," Zack asked.

Tisha looked at him, her eyes twinkling. "That was my supervisor who just spoke to your supervisor, Janice, who told her that you wreck a vehicle every other investigation. She said it's probably your fault, and the FBI would cover the cost."

"Oh, crap," Zack said. "There goes my budget again."

Eagle Feather turned to look out the window, but Zack knew he was grinning.

They changed out of their camo at Tisha's quarters, packed it away, and drank about a half gallon of water each.

"I see no point for you to hide anymore," Zack said to Eagle Feather. "Let's go get some food at the restaurant."

"How will we get there?" the Navajo asked.

Tisha dangled some keys. "The park service issued me another truck," she said.

Eagle Feather raised a brow at Zack. "The FBI never issues you a second vehicle after you destroy the first."

"They did once," Zack said.

Tisha drove to the resort. They ate a fine meal in the restaurant, then adjourned to Zack's room to plan their next step.

"I have some questions," Tisha said. "How will we get to Wingate pass? And how will we find these caves?"

"Good questions." Zack turned to his computer and brought up a topo map. He studied it, then said, "I think we can take Badwater Road to sections of the old Borax Twenty Mule Team road through Wingate Wash."

Tisha looked over his shoulder. "I don't see any road."

"It's a wash," Eagle Feather said.

Tisha looked at him, puzzled.

"He means the road will have washed out over time," Zack explained.

"Do you think my truck can manage it?" She frowned. "I don't want to wreck a second truck."

"Not even Zack has managed to do that," Eagle Feather said.

Zack ignored Eagle Feather. "We'll need a special vehicle." He drummed his fingers on the desk. "Let's see what Commander Barroff can do for us."

A call to the commander yielded just what they needed. Barroff would arrange for a helicopter to drop a vehicle with fuel and supplies near the terminus of the wash.

"This is going to be fun," Tisha said. She rubbed her hands together in excitement.

Eagle Feather did not look as pleased. "We will be sitting ducks for Maria out there."

"The assassin?" Tisha asked. "She could not possibly have survived in that truck."

Zack glanced at her. "Everyone assumes she was in the truck at the time. Why would you think she wouldn't notice that fifty-caliber gun? The second she fired her shot, she went to cover."

Tisha looked dazed. "Where, for heaven's sake?"

"Under the sand, probably, in a prepared cavity." He gave Tisha a stern look. "If we are to survive this, you must assume this killer can do everything you don't think possible. The two of us have experience with her, so we know this to be true."

"But she can't possibly know where we're going."

"There you go, assuming," Eagle Feather said.

Tisha's mood altered noticeably for the remainder of the evening. Zack loved her cheerful, upbeat nature and hated to squelch it.

They set out well before sunrise the following morning, driving south on Badwater Road, then turned right beyond Artist's Drive and crossed the valley to a road traveling down the west side of the basin. Zack kept an eye on their GPS location from time to time.

Tisha slowed when they spotted the distinct shape of Split Cinder Cone.

Zack kept a close watch on the GPS, then held up a finger. "Right here," he said.

Trisha pulled over and surveyed the expanse of the wash.

"It must be over there," Eagle Feather said, pointing to a dry channel at the north side of the volcanic plug.

Tisha engaged the four-wheel drive and drove the truck off the road and into the dry channel. Despite the truck's traction, they almost became stuck in the loose, deep sand. They progressed to the far side of the Split Cinder Cone, out of sight from the road behind the volcanic plug. Another vehicle came into view.

"It's a dune buggy!" Tisha said.

"I've heard about these," Zack said. "It's a DPV, a Desert Patrol Vehicle."

They climbed out of the truck and surrounded the skeletal buggy with its large knobby tires.

"It's got an air-cooled VW engine," Zack said, "and rear-wheel drive."

"No more air conditioning," Tisha said.

We will get plenty of air and a lot of dust," Eagle Feather said. "That is a fifty-caliber machine gun mounted in the rear."

"Maybe Maria will think twice when she sees it," Zack said. "Whoever rides in the rear gets to play with it." He glanced at Tisha. "Let's unload our gear and park your truck near those rocks. It's time to move out."

149

They found the DPV well stocked with water and MREs. Once they added their supplies, they were ready for a two-week deployment.

Zack climbed behind the wheel, and Eagle Feather sat next to him.

Tisha took the high rear seat. "Have you ever driven one of these?" she asked Zack.

"How hard could it be?" Zack said and looked at her. "Have you ever fired one of those?"

"How hard could it be?" she said.

"Oh, boy," Eagle Feather grunted.

The engine noise was surprisingly quiet at startup. But once Zack popped the clutch, the two hundred horsepower engine jumped the vehicle forward, its rear wheels churning dust.

"Whoa, there," Eagle Feather said. "We should not leave dust signals announcing our presence."

"Sorry," Zack said. "I'll get a handle on this."

Before long, they were cruising smoothly along the sand bed. The DPV's metal roof provided shade as the sun rose, but the air moving through the open vehicle warmed quickly.

The DPV handled everything they encountered in the dry bed, and when it petered out, they drove across the wash until they found another bed to follow, but every course they chose narrowed and steepened.

"Where are we?" Tisha asked.

Zack glanced at her, seated high in the observer seat with her blonde hair streaming in the breeze.

"We are in the Wingate Wash proper," Zack said over his shoulder, turning his eyes back on the terrain. "It will take us to the pass eventually, but it is a long way."

The sun's heat increased, and the team's faces glistened with sweat.

"Drink all the water you need," Zack said. "We have plenty."

He glanced at Tisha. "Especially you. You are closest to the engine's heat."

The buggy churned up a narrow trough to a ridge and began a long descent.

"Can you believe the Borax Twenty Mule teams pulled those big wagons up here?" Zack asked.

"To be accurate, they had eighteen mules and two horses that were the wheelers, hitched closest to the wagon," Tisha said.

"Why horses?"

"They are larger and stronger and could withstand the hitch and get the wagon started." She laughed. "But the mules were smarter and more adapted to the desert."

"What did they do for water?" Eagle Feather asked.

"They had one wagon called the 'Tank' to carry just water, but they would still have to refill at springs along the way."

"How many wagons made the trip?" Eagle Feather asked.

"A minimum of three," Tisha said. "The first wagon was the trailer, the second was 'the tender' or the 'back action', as they called it, and the tank wagon brought up the rear. A caravan of three wagons was a hundred and eighty feet long, and two-thirds of that was to support the first wagon."

"And yet it was still profitable," Zack asked, wonder in his voice.

"They're still selling the stuff."

Zack stopped the vehicle to pull his bandana up over his mouth. Dust and the dry air made speaking difficult, and it was uncomfortably warm now.

"Let me have that," Tisha said. She took his bandana and tied it back for him a moment later.

Zack realized she had soaked it with water. He felt new coolness from it and breathing with it made his throat less sore.

"It won't last long," Tisha said, "but I'll soak it whenever you want."

"Chief gunner and nurse," Zack said in appreciation. "What would we do without you?"

CHAPTER TWENTY-SIX

The first hours of their journey, where the wash was wide, saw wasted time backtracking and searching for a better route after the particular dry bed they had chosen dead ended with an impassable obstruction. But where the wadi narrowed between rock extrusions, the route choice was clear, and they made better time.

"How about a lunch stop?" Tisha said. "It's almost two, and a girl has gotta pee."

"At least she didn't ask if we are there yet," Eagle Feather said.

Zack found a place near a high enough bank to offer some relief from the sun and parked the DPV. When the engine died, the silence was unearthly.

"You can have this space in the shade," Zack told Tisha. "Eagle Feather and I will climb up this bank and look around for a while."

It felt good to move after the jostling, muscle-tensing ride. Above the wash, the two men surveyed an array of grey-brown dune-like prominences.

"I never realized brown came in so many hues," Zack said.

Eagle Feather waved an arm. "This is a geologist's dreamscape," he said. "It's all about tectonics."

Zack remembered Eagle Feather had taken college courses in geology.

"What does it say to you?" Zack asked.

Instead of answering, Eagle Feather gripped his arm. "It's time to go back down," he said.

Zack saw the tension on the Navajo's face and followed him off the high bank without another word.

Tisha finished adjusting her belt as they clambered down, kicking up dust from the soft bank.

"Jeez, you could give a girl a little more time."

Zack turned to Eagle Feather. "Okay, what was it?"

"I saw a flash of light near the ridgeline of one of those hills, a quarter mile away, a momentary reflection of the sun off something moving. We need to go."

Without a word, Zack climbed back in the driver's seat and started up the DPV.

Eagle Feather waved Tisha into her seat, and they were underway.

"I've had longer stops in airplanes," Tisha said.

Eagle Feather turned to look at her. "We are being followed."

"Oh." All her banter died.

Zack felt for her, knowing how utterly vulnerable and helpless she must feel. He had known they could become targets in this environment where the stalker held every advantage. But reality, when it does intrude, is always considerably more poignant. He turned his head toward Tisha to say something consoling but found her reading a booklet.

"What is that?" Zack asked, astonished.

"It's an owner's manual for the fifty-caliber machine gun."

"Oh." Zack exchanged glances with Eagle Feather. "Good to know."

"You should keep your eyes on the road, White Man," Eagle Feather said.

"What road?"

"That is my point."

As he spoke, the front right wheel of the DPV dropped into a large hole, causing the entire vehicle to shudder, but true to its design, it torqued and bounced out of the depression and surged forward, its rear wheels spinning.

Zack felt suitably abashed and sent a chastened look toward the Navajo. But his friend was looking away to the right.

Eagle Feather pointed. "Try going over there," he said. "I think that might be a road."

"Wouldn't that be nice," Zack said with a sigh. He turned the vehicle, driving it out of the ever-narrowing bed and through mesquite sand fissures in the direction the Navajo pointed.

Much to their delight, it was indeed a road or at least a set of hard-packed ruts evidencing travel by other vehicles over time.

Zack turned on to it, and they picked up speed. All those random, unexpected holes and ridges were a thing of the past. It was not a two-wheel drive road by any means—

–even a standard four-wheel-drive vehicle might have had difficulty—but for the DPV, it was a walk in the park.

The sun was at its hottest. They drank water frequently, but it was as if the liquid evaporated the moment they swallowed it. Zack's skin felt like sandpaper gritting against his clothing, his arm and leg muscles ached from tension and his attempts to stay balanced, and his butt felt like one massive bruise. The relative smoothness of this track was blissful.

They passed out of the surrounding hills into an open flatland where stone pinnacles thrust up like bad teeth, evidence of magma intrusions millions of years ago since uncovered by erosion. Beyond the flatland, the terrain ascended and became jagged and crusty, the color of stale gingerbread.

Zack turned off the DPV and surveyed the land ahead. The engine made snapping noises as it cooled.

"We'll be easy targets for a long time out there," he said.

"Aren't we ahead of her," Tisha asked. "She couldn't possibly be keeping up. There isn't even a road off in the direction you saw the reflection."

"She is an expert on a dirt bike," Zack said. "And she would know the terrain."

"How could she?" Tisha asked. 'Isn't she this globe-trotting assassin?"

"She grew up in the Mojave Desert less than two hundred miles from here," Eagle Feather said. "She is the daughter of a Chemehuevi Runner and inherited all his skills. She knows this desert like the back of her hand."

"Oh."

"What have you learned about that gun?" Zack asked.

"I think I know to fire it, but I haven't read the part about loading it."

"Is it loaded now, do you know?"

"I think so. There are bullets dangling from it."

The heat closed in like a furnace. The desert basin beyond was hidden by shimmers.

"With luck, the heat distortion will prevent her from sighting in on us," Zack said.

The Navajo nodded his approval. "No choice. We have to go."

"I will change speeds often to make us a difficult target. Tisha, get ready to fire that gun. Watch the area behind and to the south of us."

"How can I shoot at her if I can't see her?"

"Eagle Feather will be your spotter. Watch him."

"The fifty caliber won't have the effective range of the sniper rifle she will be using," Eagle Feather said. "But it might make her keep her head down until we can get across. She won't be expecting it."

"Enough talk," Zack said. "Is everyone ready? Fasten your seatbelts!"

CHAPTER TWENTY-SEVEN

Zack slipped the clutch, the DPV lurched forward, then gained speed. Eagle Feather removed his harness and climbed into the rear near Tisha's seat to get her attention if he needed it. The noise from the engine increased along with vibration throughout the vehicle's metal frame as it leaped and bounded.

Dust enveloped the vehicle and lifted as a rising cloud behind them. Zack felt they were airborne more than they were on solid ground, causing the steering control to disappear at those times until the front wheels slammed back to earth.

Dust sifted into his eyes through the sides of his sunglasses, but he dared not release a hand from the steering wheel. He gave up trying to miss the smaller lumps and bumps on the rough track and concentrated instead on avoiding the most sinister holes and obstacles.

His goal became a group of large rock protrusions forming a gateway to a ridge. Once there, they could hide out of view of the sniper. That goal remained elusive. Distances in the desert were hard to calculate; the clear air rendered objects closer than they were. But damn! It was taking too long.

Zack slowed suddenly, swerved to one side, then sped up, attempting to disrupt the shooter's aim. Gasps and grunts came from his passengers as they hung on.

The road dipped and rose again, and the distance to his goal had diminished. Zack counted each yard they traveled without a bullet striking them as a victory. He gave the DPV more gas. The buggy skittered sideways, straightened, and roared on.

The sudden hammer-like percussion of the fifty-caliber gun rattled Zack's eardrums. Eight reports sounded in milliseconds before the gun went silent. Tisha had shot her load.

"Where?" Eagle Feather yelled.

Tisha hollered something Zack couldn't hear. He drove on.

"Reload!" the Navajo said.

"I don't know how!" Tisha yelled back.

Zack became aware of Eagle Feather moving. Then the DPV hit a rut, and the vehicle lurched into the air. Eagle Feather flew up and slammed down between the front bucket seats.

"You can't get to her," Zack yelled.

"Thank you for your encouragement, White Man."

Eagle Feather moved out of his peripheral vision. Zack slowed and stopped swerving. If the Navajo fell out, their problems would increase.

The sheer wall of a rock formation loomed ahead, and then they were in its shadow, and Zack turned from the track to under its lee and into shade. He turned off the motor. The stillness was stunning.

Eagle Feather clutched the vehicle frame with his head against Tisha's knee. The fifty-caliber machine gun pointed hard left. Tisha gripped it with both hands, white-knuckled. The dangling ribbon of bullets was gone.

159

"Is everyone okay?" Zack asked.

Eagle Feather grunted and untangled himself. Tisha stared wide-eyed, her mouth forming a soundless 'O'.

"What did you see?" the Navajo asked.

Tisha was unable to reply at once. She came to life slowly. Her eyes looped from one to the other as if she'd never seen them before.

"I didn't see anything," she said. "It just went off by itself." Her finger still gripped the trigger.

"So. All for nothing."

Eagle Feather climbed out of the vehicle and stood testing his joints. "Maybe not," he said. "Just when you hit that bump, I thought I saw a flash to the southeast."

Zack climbed out and joined Eagle Feather. Every muscle ached. He found he was shaking from adrenaline.

"How far away was the flash?"

"I could not tell."

"Tisha, are you okay?" Zack asked.

"I think so," she said. "I'm sorry I wasted those bullets. We hit a bump, the gun lifted, and my finger was on the trigger. Every bullet was gone before I even realized it was firing."

Eagle Feather's eyes traveled along the buggy's frame. "The flashes from the machine gun might have helped Maria zero in her aim," he said. His gaze went to the spare tire lashed to the front of the vehicle. He pointed. "Look there."

A glint of metal showed in the knobby tread of the tire. Zack looked close. "That's a bullet. It just caught the edge of the tire tread."

He studied the DPV. "When we hit that bump, the nose lifted. Otherwise, this bullet might have hit Tisha. We got lucky."

Tisha stood unsteadily next to the vehicle, her face white.

Zack handed around a water bottle. "Drink up, everyone, and rest for a moment. Tisha, start reading. Learn how to load that gun. We're going to need it." He began to walk away. "Eagle Feather, let's see if we can determine where Maria's shot came from."

They walked along the base of the rock pinnacle to where the soft ground steepened and opened to a view of the flat basin beyond and the ripple of multi-hued hills to the south.

"The flash was near that first hill to the left," the Navajo said.

"That's got to be a mile away."

"That explains why the bullet didn't pass through the tire."

"Helluva shot."

"Yes."

The two men stood in silence. Each respected the killer who pursued them and realized the dangers ahead.

"Listen!" Eagle Feather tilted an ear. "Do you hear that?"

Zack shook his head.

"Turn your ear toward the rock surface. It acts as a sounding board."

Zack did but still heard nothing. Then he did hear something, a faint chainsaw-like sound. He knew the sound, the whining complaint of a motorbike, so distant they almost missed it.

"It's Maria," Zack said. "She's on the move."

Eagle Feather nodded.

They turned as one and walked back to the DPV. Tisha sat in the driver's seat, reading the machine gun manual.

"I know how to do this," she said. "It looks simple, but I'll need your help. Those bullet belts are ridiculously heavy."

Tisha was right. The process was simple, a matter of fitting the first shell correctly and cocking the gun three times until the top of the link emerged. They found a loader tray and attached it to the machine gun. It would allow more ammo to feed through without having to reload.

"Would you prefer Eagle Feather operate the gun?" Zack asked Tisha.

She stared at him with fire in her eyes. "No way! I got this."

"You got it."

Zack consulted his computer map before starting the vehicle.

"This indicates the road should improve in another few miles," he said. "Then we'll have the advantage of speed. We need to reach the pass first. The terrain ahead is hilly and should protect us from any more ambush attempts." He gave a wry smile. "We'll figure out what to do next once we get there."

Neither man mentioned hearing the motorbike to Tisha.

CHAPTER TWENTY-EIGHT

Refreshed by the rest and plenty of water, the team churned on. Eagle Feather kept a wary eye to the south, where the sound of the motorbike had originated.

Zack guessed their pursuer must know their destination and would have a plan. Their advantage was a better road, but their pursuer had a better knowledge of the terrain.

Their route improved abruptly from ruts to an actual dirt road, and the DPV picked up speed.

"Not long now," Zack shouted.

They passed the first signs of prospecting and mineral mining, some derelict wooden structures perched on slopes, precarious and forlorn. The wash they had followed for so long grew narrow and sometimes seemed to disappear.

"What are we looking for?" Tisha shouted.

"I don't know," Zack yelled back. "Anything that looks new or unusual."

The road climbed hills that rose softly to either side, with scattered rocks and dried brush, nothing on the windswept landscape tall enough to hide even a coyote. Zack stopped the vehicle where the long descent to the west began. His altimeter read just over three thousand feet.

"We are on the pass summit," he said.

"There's absolutely nothing here," Tisha said.

"We need another look at the topo map."

"But not here," Eagle Feather said.

"Right. We need concealment. I'll drive down the western slope and take the next side road we find."

It turned out to be a half mile, a dirt road used by heavy trucks in the past, judging from the size of the tracks.

"Some of those tire tracks here look fresh," Eagle Feather said.

"There might be an active mine down this road," Tisha said.

"These tracks are too small for an ore truck," Zack said. "It must be a pickup or an SUV."

The ungraded road followed the hill contour, then dropped into a basin with high desert flora surrounded by abrupt hills with jagged rock spires.

Zack stopped in the shelter of one of the spires. He checked the map.

"We are beyond the Death Valley National Park border and firmly inside Navy property." He pointed ahead. "This road leads to an old mine, but according to this map, it isn't active anymore."

"So why the fresh tire tracks?" Tisha asked.

"Good question. And that is what we came here to find: indications of recent activity." Zack grinned at them. "Shall we proceed?"

Eagle Feather indicated the land ahead. "There is not much cover there."

"Not much cover anywhere."

Eagle Feather shrugged.

"Going ahead is better than sitting and waiting for the killer," Tisha said.

"Off we go, then," Zack said. With a spurt of dust, the DPV picked up speed. The road surface was solid here, and the buggy flew as if on a freeway. In just minutes, they were in the shadow of towers of jumbled rock.

The dust they created hung suspended above their route, providing a neon sign for the sniper who stalked them to follow.

The road climbed into a narrow canyon as the landscape changed dramatically to steep fields beneath vertical buttresses. The layered cliffs were turned at an angle by the forces of nature, exposing well-defined strata. This terrain was every prospector's dream.

The canyon widened, then ended in a circle of craggy rock pillars, each with a skirt of stone debris. On the steep slope were two wooden structures, one a hundred feet above the other, clinging as if glued there, with wall boards askew and leaning timbers, slowly capitulating to the inevitable destruction of time.

The upper structure had a skeletal roof line interrupted by a square, chimney-like protrusion. Behind the building stood a wooden sluice on stilts.

The nearer structure sat upon a stone foundation, which had preserved it better, keeping it level on the sloping terrain. It appeared to be in far better repair.

"This is the work shed and miners' quarters," Tisha said. "The upper building is the shaft and housing for the winch."

"This mine must not have been operational for a hundred years," Zack said.

The road ended as they neared the buildings. The nose of a pickup truck protruded from the far side of the building.

"Someone is here. Tisha, bring the fifty around to bear on the lower building, just in case," Zack said.

"Aye, aye, captain."

Eagle Feather picked up a rifle and lay it across his lap.

Zack drove forward at a crawl. They saw no sign of life. The pickup truck came into full view. It was a recent model. There was no one in it.

Zack parked facing the truck leaving the motor running. A coating of dirt over the truck's white paint showed it had traveled the road recently. In its bed was a bulky plastic-wrapped bundle.

The building walls displayed evidence of recent attempts to patch them. Canvas covered a window as if to keep out the light for sleeping.

Zack revved the engine. They waited, but no one appeared.

"I guess we'll have to flush them out."

"They could be down the shaft," Eagle Feather said.

"I'll take a look in this building." Zack glanced at Tisha. "Keep watch. Maria could come along anytime."

Zack climbed out of the buggy, checked his handgun, and walked to the truck. He saw keys in the ignition and maps on the passenger seat. A pickaxe, sledgehammer, and other prospector tools were in the truck bed. The plastic-wrapped bundle sat on a pallet. From its size, Zack judged it to be a large generator.

Everything suggested a lone prospector. He saw no weapons. He walked to the door of the shed and knocked.

There was no answer, no noise from inside. The door had a latch. Zack lifted it and slid the door open. The interior was dark after the brilliant sunshine outside, and Zack waited for his eyes to adjust. The only light filtered into the room from gaps in the walls.

As his vision adjusted, he saw a cot with a sleeping bag, an open suitcase on the floor next to it, a folding table with cookware and a gasoline stove, and in the middle of the room, a large table built of timbers similar to the wood framing of the shed. Maps and paper with hand-sketched diagrams lay spread open on it.

Someone was staying here and might be in the shaft. Or he might be somewhere among the rocks, watching them. Zack had seen no weapons in the truck or the shed, but the man could have a rifle with him.

Sudden percussive raps from the machine gun outside startled Zack. He rushed to the door. Tisha had the big gun trained up the hillside beyond the shed. Eagle Feather was standing next to the DPV, holding his rifle.

Zack looked up the slope. A man in coveralls knelt near the shaft building with his hands raised high. He looked terrified.

CHAPTER TWENTY-NINE

"What happened?" Zack asked. He looked at Tisha. "Why did you shoot?"

She looked a little abashed. "That man suddenly appeared up there. I just fired a couple of rounds over his head."

"I think she likes to play with that gun," Eagle Feather said.

Zack was not amused. "You've announced our presence to the entire area," he said. He waved for the man to come down, calling to him. "We won't hurt you."

The man rose hesitantly to his feet and came down the slope. He was tall and broad-shouldered, with a ruddy face and sandy hair streaked with grey. He wore coveralls and dusty boots.

"Who are you?" he asked as he neared. "You scared the shit out of me."

Zack pulled his credentials. "I am Agent Zack Tolliver with the FBI. We are investigating a conspiracy, and we need your help. What is your name?"

"Brett. Brett Rackwell. This is my claim."

"It doesn't look like it's been worked in a while."

Rackwell shook his head and wiped sweat from his brow. "It's been in my family for a couple of generations. I thought about starting it up again just lately."

"What are you mining?"

Rackwell took on a wary look. "Is that germane to your investigation?"

"It could be. Someone is interested enough in something in this area to commit murder."

"Could we talk in the shade?" Tisha asked. "It's too hot out here."

Rackwell glanced at her. "Sure, lady. Anything to get you away from that gun. We can go inside."

They followed Rackwell into the building.

"I'm short on chairs," he said, "but you can sit on the cot or those boxes if you want." He turned to Zack. "Can you tell me anything more about your investigation? I haven't killed anybody if that's what this is about."

Zack nodded. "The long and short of it is, someone hired an assassin to kill a scientist we think was on his way to this area. His body got dumped over in Death Valley. We want to know why he wanted to come here. That's why I'm asking what you are mining."

Rackwell gave his head a slow shake. "There's nothing here to excite anybody wanting to get rich. My grandpappy found a little gold, but that played out quickly and never did assay high enough for the effort." His eyes narrowed at Zack. "What kind of scientist was this guy who got murdered?"

"Supposedly a fuel expert," Zack said.

Rackwell crossed his arms. "We got one element out here that might have interested him. Lithium." He looked out from under bushy eyebrows. "Not exactly fuel, but it will make a car go."

"You found lithium?" Eagle Feather asked, studying Rackwell's face.

"Is that why you came out here?" Zack asked him.

Rackwell looked abashed. "Well, I heard the ore was out here. I thought I'd take a look. America produces just one percent of the world's lithium, and believe me, its value will skyrocket. You'll see countries like Australia, China, and Chile begin to control the market just like the Arabs did with the oil."

"Why is it so valuable?" Tisha asked.

Rackwell looked at her strangely. "You been living under a rock, lady? Lithium is the major component of car batteries. Companies that manufacture EVs can't get enough of it. The manufacture of gasoline-powered vehicles will probably end in the next two decades."

"Oh."

Eagle Feather eyed Rackwell. "Have you found any?"

The miner's face took on a shrewd expression. "Maybe I did, maybe I didn't."

Zack glanced at Rackwell. "What does the ore look like? Is it hard to recognize?"

"You can find lithium in pegmatite, but also in brine. For that, you pump brine water out of the ground and let it sit in the sun in ponds until the lithium separates. Then you process it with soda ash and other purification processes. Takes a couple of years."

"How much water does it require?"

"About five hundred thousand gallons to make a metric ton of lithium."

"Geez, that's a lot of water," Tisha said.

"How is lithium processed from pegmatite?" Zack asked.

"That process is expensive. It requires roasting, calcination, and leaching in various ways."

"Supposing you did find lithium-bearing ore, would it be worth it to mine, given the expense?" Eagle Feather asked.

Rackwell shrugged. "Not right now. But it's all about the market. If the market grows enough, it will become worth it."

"It's hard to imagine someone hiring an assassin to kill a scientist over a possible market for lithium," Zack said.

Rackwell watched the three of them, his eyes questioning. "You think there is something else going on here?"

"Yes, but we don't know what it is," Zack said. "It is something worth taking great risks."

"Something worth killing for," Tisha added.

"And you think this something is out here somewhere?"

Zack nodded. "Somewhere in this area." He waved an encompassing arm. "The only place the murdered scientist could have been going is the Wingate Pass area."

"And the killer would not have followed us out here otherwise," Tisha added.

"Out here?" Rackwell's composure slipped a bit.

"We may have put you in some danger," Zack said. "We'll be leaving soon."

"Would this killer come after me?"

"Not unless you know something you haven't told us," Eagle Feather said.

Rackwell spread his big hands. "That's it. That's all of it. I've been out here just a few weeks, looking for spodumene, petalite, lepidolite, amblygonite, or any other igneous inclusions that might contain lithium in any quantity. I've been down in the shaft most of that time."

"Have you seen or heard anything unusual in that time?" Zack asked. "Talked to anybody? Visited neighboring mines?"

Rackwell gave an ironic grin. "Prospectors are not exactly a tea clutch group." He paused, thinking. "There was one thing, though, a little while back. It was a loud bang, like a sonic boom or an earthquake. It woke me up and shook the entire building. I thought this old place would come down around me. I ran outside and got in the truck in case of an aftershock, but it didn't happen. Just that one bang. That was it."

He shrugged. "Next day, I drove out to the pass to see what I could see, thinking maybe there was a mine explosion nearby or something like that. There was nothing, but a few other people had come out for the same reason. We yacked about it for a while, but nobody knew anything."

Rackwell spread his arms again. "That was it. It was the only time I have spoken to anyone since I came here." He grimaced. "And now you, of course."

CHAPTER THIRTY

"How can you own a mine in a military reservation?" Tisha asked.

Rackwell smiled. "That's pretty simple. We were here first. The mine is patented. All the mines around here are patented."

Don't they test ordinance out here?"

"Sure. But the Navy knows we are here and stick to other parts of their range. There is always the risk of an errant bomb, of course. But most of the time, we're underground anyway."

"How was that big bang you described different from errant ordnance?" Zack asked.

Rackwell scratched his chin. "It just was. It was much stronger than anything I'd experienced before. We hear them all the time, kind of muffled booms, you know? But this was huge and made the ground shake. And, it was at night."

Zack was doing calculations in his head. "You said this big boom was a while ago?" he asked, looking at Rackwell, who nodded.

"Maybe four, five days. You lose track out here."

Zack turned to Eagle Feather. "That would have been before the Navy hired you."

"Yes."

"You're wondering if the two things are connected," Tisha said, growing excited.

Zack nodded. "Something went boom, and then a scientist comes onto the navy base where the boom happened, and he disappears while headed in this direction. Coincidence? I don't think so."

"We need to find out what made the boom," Tisha said.

"Could you pinpoint the direction of the noise?" Eagle Feather asked Rackwell.

He shook his head. "No. As I said, it woke me up. It sounded like it was all around me, like thunder."

"It must have detonated in the air," Zack said. "Did you hear any sounds preceding it?"

"Again, I was asleep...but wait a minute! I think I did hear something like a sizzle just before the boom unless I dreamt it. Something like a steak on the grill but louder."

"Well, if it burst in the air somewhere, how will we find any evidence of it?" Tisha asked.

"Ordinarily, I'd say it would be impossible," Zack said. He stepped toward the table crowded with maps and papers and scanned them. "But someone sent an expert out here. Why? It had to be to recover something. So something hit the ground. And they must have thought it would be large enough for someone to find."

Zack glanced at Rackwell. "Are these topo maps of this area? "

The prospector nodded and joined Zack. "You want the Wingate Pass Quadrant?"

"You tell me. If you had to specify the direction of the blast in very general terms of East, West, North, or South, how would you respond?"

He shrugged. "Jesus, man, I just don't know."

"Okay, how about the sizzle? Coming toward you or going away?"

"Ah, yeah. Coming toward me."

"From where?"

"There." Rackwell pointed southwest.

"Now we're getting somewhere. Let's look at the Wingate Pass quadrant and the next one to the southwest."

Rackwell shuffled through the maps and spread one out on the table. "This is the USGS 7.5-minute series of Wingate Pass. If you want a general overview, this is what you want."

Zack leaned over it. "Go back in your memory, listen to the sizzling sound, and draw a line toward it and a circle around the area you would guess the boom encompassed. Can you do that?"

"It's gonna be a big circle, but here goes." Rackwell drew a short line to the southwest and then a circle. He was right. It was a big circle.

He looked up at Zack. "I don't see how that will help you much."

"It's a start," Zack said. He grabbed his phone and pushed a button. After a few rings, Janice answered.

"Hi, Janice. Can you get me a couple of satellite images? Use these coordinates." Zack read them from the map. "I need images from six days ago and another from today, covering the same area. I need the best surface detail possible."

"Are you asking me for a favor while I pay for another destroyed vehicle, Zack?"

"Come on, now, Janice. You made the offer to pay for that."

"I have no doubt you were involved in its destruction somehow, and we need to keep up good relations with all the other federal agencies. But don't worry. It will go on your budget."

Zack was silent.

Janice continued in her normal business-like tone. "I see by the signal from your sat phone you are near the coordinates you just gave me."

"Yes, I am," Zack said.

"That would place you in the middle of a naval ordnance testing area. I hope you are not there with another rented vehicle."

"Uh, no, no, not a rental...well, not exactly."

The call ended with an audible click. "*How did Janice always manage to put him on the defensive?*"

Rackwell was staring at Zack.

"What's the matter?" Zack asked him.

"You can order satellite images just like that?"

"Only because my boss knows a lot of people in helpful places," Zack said.

"Those images would be mighty useful to a prospector," Rackwell said, his tone hopeful.

Zack gave him a thoughtful look. "You might be in luck if you can help us out." He glanced at Tish and Eagle Feather. "Something caused that boom Rackwell described. My hunch is it must have left a mark." He paused. "Does anybody here know about the Tunguska explosion of 1908?"

"I do," Tisha said. "It happened in Russia. They named it for the river there."

"Wasn't that the place where all those trees got flattened?" Rackwell asked.

Tisha nodded. "That's right. It flattened an estimated eighty million trees over some eight hundred and fifty square miles and killed a lot of reindeer."

"It turned out to be a meteorite, didn't it?" Rackwell asked.

"That's right," Zack said. "Some people saw a fireball flash across the sky followed by a sound like artillery fire. The shockwave broke windows hundreds of miles away."

Rackwell stared at Zack. "This was a big boom and vibration, but nothing like you're describing."

"This might have been something on a smaller scale. But my point is it didn't have to be related to naval ordinance. It might have been something altogether different, but something that drew the interest of certain people who knew about it."

Tisha's eyes gleamed. "That might explain why Commander Barroff knew nothing about it, even though he's the base commander."

"Exactly. Then the 'fuel expert' is sent in by some interested party to check it out," Zack said.

"And when he disappears, they hire me to find him," Eagle Feather said. "It all fits."

Zack smiled. "It's a long shot, but think about the timing of events: first this boom, then this fuel expert comes along, then he is killed before he can get there. Somebody knew something about it."

"Well! I see you have almost put it all together." The soft, alluring voice came from the door where a slender figure leaned casually against the door frame, holding an AK-74 pistol like a purse.

CHAPTER THIRTY-ONE

She was a beautiful creature, half in the door shadow, the sun highlighting her raven black hair, every bit as breathtaking as Zack remembered her from their first meeting years ago. She wore loose clothing of browns and pale yellows designed to blend into a desert environment that heightened the contrast of her olive complexion and deep dark eyes peering from beneath the shadow of a desert legion cap. To Zack, she looked more youthful, vital, and appealing than ever.

"Maria!" Zack said under his breath. He felt the same surge of fear, fascination, and excitement she always caused in him.

"It is good to see you again," she said, her dark eyes on him.

For Zack, it might have been like a chance meeting in a Moroccan café with a lost love, were it not for the deadly weapon she held lightly yet expertly at her side, knowing she would use it without hesitation.

She gestured with the gun toward the Navajo. "Eagle Feather, my old foe."

"My shot did not inconvenience you too much, I hope," the Navajo said.

"No more than a hangnail," she said.

Her eyes went to Tisha. "Park Service Investigative Services Branch Special Agent Patricia Knolls. Interesting."

Tisha started to speak, but a soft venomous hiss from the assassin stopped her.

Maria's eyes flashed back to Zack. "I came to tell you the game has changed. I have new orders." Her face broke into an infectious smile. "You are safe from me for now. It seems we have a common adversary. He is out there. He is the one who will kill you." She giggled like a schoolgirl, then in a soft playground chant, said, "If he can. If he can."

Then she was gone.

Eagle Feather reached for his rifle.

Zack put up a restraining palm.

"Let her go. I believe her."

"She wants to confuse us, cause us to let our guard down."

"She could have killed us all just now, burned down this building, driven away in our desert buggy, and no one the wiser."

Eagle Feather stayed put, but his eyes smoldered.

They heard the chainsaw whine of a motorbike start up, move off, and diminish into the distance.

"Who the hell was that woman?" Rackwell's question exploded out of his chest.

They looked at him in surprise, having forgotten he was there.

"That," said Zack, "is probably the world's foremost assassin."

"What is she doing here? What did she mean about not killing you and that somebody else will kill you? What's going on?"

"Take it easy," Zack said. "None of this involves you. You are quite safe."

"But what does it all mean?" Tisha asked.

"Whoever Maria works for has decided to leave us alive for now. But there is a competitor who may not be so considerate."

"Meaning another hired killer who wants us dead," Eagle Feather said.

"Is that better or worse?" Tisha asked.

Zack grimaced. "Overall, I'd say worse. Maria is the best, but at least we know something about her. This second killer is a complete unknown."

"Maria called him an adversary," Eagle Feather said. "If she is hunting him, that is good."

"What now?" Tisha asked.

"I think our best plan is to stay here and wait for the satellite images from Janice. Once we have those, we can consider our next move," Zack said.

"Aren't we sitting ducks for this other killer?" Tisha asked.

"This may be our safest place," Eagle Feather said.

"Why?"

Zack explained. "Maria knows we are here. We are the bait in her trap to draw in the other killer."

Tisha did not look convinced.

"If Maria's orders are to keep us alive, we are as safe here as anywhere," Zack said.

"Until her orders change," Eagle Feather said.

Zack's phone vibrated. He glanced at it and put it to his ear.

"Hello, Janice."

"Zack, we have the images, and I've saved you some trouble. We ran both images through a computer to find any discrepancies between them. We found one. I circled it. I'm sending the photos to you now. Good luck."

Moments later, the images arrived on his phone.

"Janice just did all our work for us," Zack said. He glanced at Rackwell. "Do you have a computer? It would be nice to see these up on a larger screen."

"Yes, I do. It's in my truck." Rackwell started to walk to the door, but Zack stopped him.

"We need to tread a bit carefully. Where is it in the truck?"

"On the front seat."

Zack nodded toward Eagle Feather, who went to the door and slid out. Two minutes later, he was back with the computer.

Zack sent the images to Rackwell.

"Go to the second image," Zack said.

Everyone crowded around the laptop while he searched for the circled anomaly. He found it and zoomed in.

"What is that?" Tisha asked.

"I'm not sure," Rackwell said. "It looks like an impact crater."

Zack stared at the screen, comparing the two images. That crater was not there before."

"It has to be from whatever exploded that night. What else could it be?" Rackwell asked.

"Where is that crater from here?" Zack asked.

Rackwell zoomed out and studied the landscape. He then rolled out a topo map and put down a finger. "It's right here, just southwest of the Wingate Pass summit.

"Do you think this is where the fuel specialist was trying to go?" Tisha asked.

"It must be," Zack said.

"But before he can get there, Maria abducts him, takes him to Desolation Canyon, and kills him." Eagle Feather said.

"Why bother? I mean, why take him so far away to kill him?" Tisha asked.

"My guess is they wanted to hide where he was going," Zack said.

"That must be why someone sent Maria and that other assassin to kill me," Eagle Feather said.

"And then they eliminated anyone at the base who might know where the man had gone," Zack said. "Someone wanted to keep this crater a secret." He hesitated. "But why the change in heart now? Why decide not to kill us now that we are so close to discovering it?"

"I think Maria needs us to lead her to the crater. After that, she can kill us," Eagle Feather said.

"Ever the optimist," Zack said.

"Now we have to go to that crater, don't we?" Tisha asked, looking less than enthusiastic.

Zack nodded. "Whatever made that crater is the solution to this entire mystery. But going there will place us in great danger."

"Maybe Commander Barroff can help us," Tisha said. "After all, it's in his backyard."

Eagle Feather nodded in agreement. "A gunship can be a great deterrent to a sniper."

Zack started to reach for his phone but then hesitated. He eyed his companions. "What if Barroff wants us to do exactly the same thing that Eagle Feather suggested Maria planned to do; get us to lead him to the crater?"

"Who is neurotic now?" Eagle Feather asked.

"Do you think Maria and Barroff could be on the same team?" Tisha asked.

Zack shrugged. "I think an assassin who could take you out at any minute is enough to worry about, let alone wondering if a gunship will appear above us and pulverize us once we lead them to the crater."

"You have to trust somebody sometime," Tisha said.

"I do," Zack said. "Me."

Eagle Feather nodded. "I agree with White Man. We must do this on our own."

Zack looked at the topo map, then at Rackwell. "It's a mile and a half away, at most?"

"That's my guess."

"We can be in and out of there in no time with the buggy," Tisha said. "If anything moves on the landscape, I'll blow it away."

"Don't get too excited," Zack said. "We're not taking the buggy. We're walking."

"What? Why?"

"Think about it. Barroff lent us the DPV. If he is scheming to get us to lead him to the crater, he might have put a location device in the buggy somewhere."

"Do you think that all this time..." Tisha's eyes widened.

Zack shrugged. "We cannot discard the possibility." He turned to Rackwell. "We may need someone with your background. You don't have to get involved. It's risky. But if you're willing, we could use you."

Rackwell stared at Zack, then at the others. "Jesus! The things I get myself into." He sighed. "Okay. I'm in."

CHAPTER THIRTY-TWO

They left at dawn just as the eastern sky paled in a narrow band above the crooked teeth background of the dark mountains. Zack and Rackwell had worked out the route with the topo map. They would avoid roads, traversing hillsides single file like a band of peccaries.

Rackwell took the lead, moving silently for a big man, finding their way from his knowledge of the terrain. There could be no lights for peering at maps. He wore a big pack with a shovel and his mineral testing equipment.

Zack came second, armed with a rifle. Tisha followed him, and Eagle Feather was in the rear with his rifle. All carried water and energy bars.

They heard only the sounds of cloth against brush, the rattle of small stones sliding away, and the crunch of footfalls on soft earth. The early morning air was still. No creatures stirred, and no birds called. The smell of sage and mesquite was in the air. Zack thought it would have been a perfect morning outing were it not for the danger of sudden, deadly rifle shots.

The walk grew steep where the terrain rose toward the pass, and Zack warmed even though the sun wouldn't break free of the horizon for another half hour. By the time it did, they were on level ground, the terrain beginning to fall away.

Rackwell kept up a strong pace and seemed sure of his path. Now he paused for a water break.

"It's not far from here now," he murmured to Zack. "I think it's just beyond that ridge somewhere."

They moved on. Now the sky was streaked with the sun's searching rays, and the intensely bright sphere itself peeked over the distant skyline. The heat intensified wherever its rays struck.

Clearing the ridge, Rackwell paused to study the terrain. The mix of bright light and dark shadow caused features in the land to look flat and drew hollows where none existed.

"We should fan out now," Rackwell said. "It could be anywhere around here. From the satellite image, it seemed to be fifty feet in diameter. We should stumble right onto it."

They moved forward, spread so that each could see the others. The sun seemed in a hurry to rise now, and soon the shadows thinned and lengthened. Each minute, their surroundings became more visible. Eagle Feather stopped, raised an arm, and pointed.

Zack had seen it; a ridge of fresh dirt. They moved toward and grouped at the dirt ridge.

"Let me take a reading before we go any further," Rackwell said and lowered his pack. He reached in and removed a small radiation detector. Holding it up, he watched the screen.

"There's no significant rise in radiation detected here," Rackwell said. "Let's take a closer look."

He stepped over the outer ridge and across a flat area to a circular dirt mound about two feet high. In the middle of it was a pit.

"This is a typical impact crater," Rackwell said.

"A meteorite?" Tisha asked.

"Must be. Let's take a look." He peered into the pit with his flashlight. The crater was about three feet deep and five feet in diameter.

Something dark and metallic reflected in the glow of his flashlight. Zack took pictures of it with his phone.

"It's a chunk of metal," Tisha said.

Rackwell reached in with a gloved hand and touched its surface. "It feels rough." He took his prospecting hammer from his belt and tapped the object with it in several places, listening.

"Hear that?" he said. "It has variable densities from different metals." He dug in his pack for a chisel. "I'm going to take a couple of samples. Stand back and avert your eyes."

There came a loud pinging of the chisel on the object's surface. Eventually, Rackwell handed Zack a cracker-size sample. "I'm gonna get a couple more from different areas of the exposed surface," he said. "This will take a while. It seems to have about a millimeter of fusion crust and different metal densities beneath—I don't know, it's weird."

Fifteen minutes later, he handed Zack two more samples, then stood and stretched. He dug into his pack for a compass and held it near the black metallic object in

191

the pit. The needle immediately turned toward the specimen. "We have meteoric iron, nickel-iron, for sure," Rackwell muttered. "But there's something else going on here. It isn't just your average meteorite."

Zack looked at their surroundings. Absorbed by the meteorite, they'd not been paying attention. He felt vulnerable.

"Take the samples you need, and let's get out of here," he told Rackwell.

The sun lit them like a spotlight, and their long shadows pointed to them like giant fingers.

Eagle Feather scanned the nearby slopes.

"Someone is up there," he said.

At that moment, a shot sounded. All four dropped to the ground like a row of dominoes. The sun's glare defeated their efforts to see in its direction.

"Is anyone hit?" Zack asked.

"That shot was not at us," Eagle Feather said.

They lay still, waiting. There were no more shots.

"We can't stay here," Zack said. "We need to move out." He looked toward Eagle Feather to lead the way, but the Navajo was already gone.

Zack took over. "Follow me," he said. He jumped up and ran a zig-zag route toward a rock cluster a hundred feet away. They arrived in its shadow, one after the other, panting, hearts racing. No other shot had sounded.

"Is everyone okay?" Zack asked.

"Where's Eagle Feather?" Tisha looked around.

"Don't worry about him. He tends to disappear at times like this." He touched Rackwell's arm. "We need to get back to the mine. Lead us. Eagle Feather will find his way."

Without a word, the prospector rose from his crouch and moved off. Tisha followed, and Zack brought up the rear.

The return trip was fraught with anxiety and discomfort. The change from night chill to daytime heat had been instantaneous, and the fear of ambush was ever-present.

Their first sight of the mine structures brought relief, and once they were inside the shed walls, they collapsed in a heap.

Zack passed a water bottle around. "Drink up," he said. "We have to move out immediately. We've got to get these samples to a safe place." His eyes went to Rackwell. "You had better come with us. You won't be safe here anymore."

The prospector frowned. "But..."

"Don't worry about your holdings. It will all be over soon as soon as those samples are safe. Then you can get back to your life. But for right now, we are all in danger."

"What about Eagle Feather?" Tisha asked.

"He'll find us."

Rackwell glared at Zack. "Who's after us?" he demanded. "That woman or someone else?"

Zack's mouth tensed. "At this point, I have no idea. We have to assume everyone wants these samples." He went to the table and studied the open map. "What's the fastest way out of here?"

"There's no fast way. The road is better west of Wingate Pass. I mean, there is a road, but it's a long, long way out. Most miners use helicopters."

"What if you're right about Barroff bugging the DPV?" Tisha asked. "He could follow us wherever we go."

"You mentioned a helicopter," Zack said to Rackwell. "Where is it? Who owns it?"

"There's two of them. The Briggs outfit owns one, and some other outfits share one. Everyone else hires as needed."

"Where's this helipad?"

"About five, mebbe six miles west of the pass."

"Can you get us there in the truck?"

"Yep. But there is no guarantee any helicopters are there."

"There will be," Zack said.

CHAPTER THIRTY-THREE

"I know what you're doing." Tippy's usually confident voice sounded close to panic. "You're going to get us all killed. You don't know who you're dealing with here."

"Right now, I'm dealing with anyone who threatens my command. If that means you, so be it."

Tippy sounded miserable. "I'm not threatening you, Simon. I'm in the same vise as you. These people are powerful beyond your imaginings, and now they're pissed."

"You keep saying 'these people'," Barroff said. "It's about time you told me who they are."

"That's not going to happen. These people can get to you and me no matter how much security we surround ourselves with. Do not imagine closing down your base will keep them from getting to you."

"What do they want?"

"They want you to leave the Sweiger business alone. He was never there. He never existed. Quit helping the feds."

"And if I don't?"

"Then we're both dead men."

=

Eagle Feather followed the long shadows cast by the early sun toward the pinpoint of reflected light he saw just before the shot sounded.

There had been no more shots. Eagle Feather wanted to know who fired that solitary shot and what it meant.

Maria had said there was another killer out here. Eagle Feather knew she lied as naturally as breathing when the occasion warranted, but she may have told the truth about a second killer. In his heart, he doubted she intended to leave any of them alive.

The Navajo crept across ground that rose steadily, moving among jagged rock and cactus clumps. It was hard to estimate the distance to the flicker of light he'd seen, but he had the direction fixed in his head. He would reach that spot eventually.

It took him ten minutes. The dead man lay on his stomach, his scoped rifle still in his hands beneath him, pointed toward the crater. His death had arrived instantly from a bullet passing through the back of his head and exiting his forehead.

Eagle Feather estimated the angle of the bullet's path with his eye and gazed back along it to where the imaginary line met higher ground and saw a group of craggy rocks that likely served as cover for his killer. The Navajo went there, his rifle ready.

Maria had been there. She'd wanted him to know. He found her neat, deliberately placed footprint. She'd left no other sign, only the one she'd chosen to leave, and now she was gone, probably to follow Zack and the others.

Eagle Feather went back to the dead rifleman. He saw nothing distinctive about the man's features, nothing to suggest his nationality or race. As expected, he had nothing in his pockets and no labels on his clothing. He could have acquired his weapon anywhere in the world.

So Maria had been truthful about an adversary. She had used them as bait to draw this killer out to where she could eliminate him with a single shot. Her surprise visit to the mine now made sense. Maria had wanted them to continue their mission, to find the impact crater. She had watched them take the samples.

Eagle Feather guessed her intentions toward them would now change. Was she there to protect the secret enshrouded in this mysterious meteor? If so, she must recover the samples. That meant Zack, Tisha, and Rackwell were in great danger.

Eagle Feather studied the terrain, got his bearings, and struck off toward Rackwell's mine with a mile-eating jog.

=

Zack decided they must leave the DPV behind on the chance Barroff had bugged it, and they all clambered aboard Rackwell's pickup. He had called Janice and convinced her to dispatch a helicopter to the helipad. She readily consented when she understood their lives were in peril. The bird should reach the pad shortly before they did in the pickup, according to Rackwell's estimation.

Zack and Tisha rode in the truck bed with rifles ready.

"What about Eagle Feather?" Tisha asked.

Zack didn't look at her. "We must get these samples to safety, no matter what. Eagle Feather chose to protect our rear and help us escape. If we wait for him, it will all be for nothing." He added, more for himself than her, "He'll make it. He always does."

=

At that moment, Eagle Feather was climbing the south side of the pass, skirting the cacti and needle-point agave. The sun was fully up and unrelenting, and sweat coursed through the grime on his body.

He could not guess Zack's plans. Would he wait at the mine buildings or immediately begin the return trip to Death Valley?

He had to reach the mine road turnoff before they left it. It was his only chance to intercept them. He angled his run to approach west of the pass summit. The Navajo guessed he was an hour behind them.

When he arrived at the intersection, he studied the tracks and, to his relief, saw that the DPV had not returned this way. So they had not left yet. The Navajo trotted down the road.

He became aware of a mosquito-like hum in his ear. It grew louder and became the angry chainsaw sound of a mountain bike. Eagle Feather eyed the surrounding terrain for cover, saw a shallow arroyo, and sprinted off the road.

He dropped into it and lay flat with his rifle aimed toward the roadway.

The bike's engine grew louder, hiccupping as gears changed on steeper sections, then sounded suddenly close. The Navajo realized Maria was not on the road. She was somewhere behind him.

The two-cycle engine's whine abruptly died to a steady put-put, idling somewhere up the slope to his rear. Eagle Feather dared not turn to look and lay still. Could she see him from her position? Would the next thing he felt be the punch of a bullet?

Still, the engine idled.

Eagle Feather waited, frozen in position. Was Maria playing with him? Was she waiting for him to react? He wondered if he would hear the sound of her laughter just before she pulled the trigger.

But then there was another noise; the wheezing rumble of a vintage truck. Zack and his companions were coming. That was why she was waiting.

There was no time. The truck would appear around the corner any moment now. Maria would shoot the driver or the tires, and the pickup would run off the road, and it would all be over.

Eagle Feather was helpless.

A stone, smooth and rounded by weather, lay near his hand. The Navajo grasped it. He knew there was no time to sit up, turn, and aim his rifle. The stone would do little, even if he could send it anywhere near her with only sound to guide his aim, but it was the only thing he could do. He waited, watching the empty road where the truck must appear.

CHAPTER THIRTY-FOUR

The Navajo tensed and waited, and the truck sound, with its slight worn-valve wheezing, changed from far off to immediate as it rounded the corner. Eagle Feather came up to a knee and whipped the stone toward the killer.

His mind snapped an image of a helmeted figure straddling the bike, weight on the back foot, rifle aligned toward the truck, then the figure intuitively sensing the motion of the Navajo below, the helmeted head turning toward him while the rock arced and landed in the dirt next to the bike's front wheel in a spurt of dust, the rifle knocked off course.

As soon as he'd released the rock, Eagle Feather continued turning and brought up his rifle. He'd gained a few milliseconds with surprise. In those same milliseconds, Maria gunned the bike, steering one-handed, the rifle in the other, and disappeared over the ridge.

Eagle Feather turned to look at the truck. It was passing from view up the grade, Zack and Tisha in the bed, conversing. They'd never known their danger.

He'd denied Maria her first attempt, but she was gone now and would have more opportunities. The truck was gone too, its occupants unaware of their friend left standing there.

He slumped and squatted on the hot roadway, frustrated. Maria would follow the noisy truck, ambush it, kill the occupants, and once she had the samples, be gone forever. The Navajo had no doubt that was her mission. She wouldn't even bother with him. He no longer stood in her way. Leaving him helpless and useless was as good as killing him. She'd be satisfied with that.

Then something clicked in his mind. They'd chosen to take Rackwell's truck. That meant the DPV was at the mine. There was still a chance!

=

The truck roared into the intersection at Wingate Pass Road and skidded into a right turn without slowing. Dust erupted around them.

"I guess everyone knows where we are by now," Zack said, watching it rise like steam from a geyser.

"They have to catch us first," Tisha said. The truck accelerated on the better road.

Zack slid open the cab window. "How far is it from here?" he yelled.

"About three miles," came the answer. "But the road gets better." Rackwell picked up more speed.

"Don't go too fast," Zack yelled. "An accident won't help." The truck was going air born from the bumps.

As they hurtled down the road, dust obscured everything behind them and seeped up from beneath. Zack and Tisha clung to the side rail to keep themselves aboard.

They could hear little beyond the rusted old muffler roar, the banging of worn springs, and the squeal of metal against metal as the truck bed torqued. Then, without warning, the truck pitched to the right, veered off the road into a ditch, choked, snorted, and died.

Zack and Tisha slammed against the cab. When he recovered, Zack slid the window open.

"I told you to slow down. What's the matter with you!"

He saw Rackwell slumped forward against the steering wheel with his head at a strange angle. Blood seeped from beneath his cap, matting his hair. He realized what had happened.

"Get out!" he yelled. He leaped over the rail and crouched near the truck, clutching his rifle. Tisha came rolling over the side and nearly landed on top of him.

"Where's your rifle?"

Tisha gestured back up at the truck bed.

"Shit."

Zack heard a voice call out. It was a familiar voice.

"Checkmate, Zack."

Zack tried to get a fix on Maria's location. She was somewhere out in front of the truck. He put a hand on Tisha's arm.

"No matter what she says, don't move."

The voice came again, calm, reassuring. "Give me those samples, Zack. That's all I want."

Zack kept his hand on Tish's arm.

"Stalling won't help you, Zack. Eagle Feather isn't coming."

Zack's stomach scrunched as if a hand had clutched him there. Eagle Feather wouldn't be coming! He didn't doubt her. She lied when it suited her, yet pride was involved in her duels with the Navajo. The sound of it rang in her voice.

"I have all the time in the world, Zack. I have no reason to kill either of you once I have those samples. But if you resist...well, that changes things."

"They're right here in the truck," Zack shouted. "Help yourself."

A peel of laughter rang out. "I'd rather you serve me," Maria said. "Or, you could send out the girl with them."

Zack's grip tightened on Tisha's arm.

"We're both quite comfortable right where we are," Zack said.

"Pardon me if I doubt that."

This time her voice sounded from a slightly different location.

"She's on the move," Zack whispered. "She'll try to get a line of sight to us. Watch your side. If you see any movement, tell me."

Zack's view was of brush-spackled terrain behind and above him and a narrow strip of roadway seen from beneath the truck. If she rushed them, he'd have almost no time to react.

She was moving because she could not see them, either. What would she do next? Rush them, or wait them out?

Time went by. Maria did not speak again. They had no way of knowing what she was doing. The sun bore down. At least they were in the truck's shade at the moment. But they had no water. He knew they could not last long.

Tisha nudged him. She gestured behind them. "I just saw a bird fly off," she said.

Zack nodded and turned his rifle to that side. "If she comes, it'll be in a rush," he said. "Get as flat to the ground as possible."

Tisha nodded.

Then they were startled by the sound of a rifle and the clang of metal on the other side of the truck. Another shot and clang sounded as a second bullet struck the vehicle in the same place.

"What's she doing?" Tisha asked, panic in her voice.

"She's either trying to ricochet a bullet off the road below the truck to hit us or..."

"Or what?'

"Or hit the fuel tank."

"Oh, God!"

Another bullet smacked the truck.

"Will the truck explode?" Tisha asked.

"Maybe, maybe not. But I think this is an attempt to get us to run. Maria is an excellent shot, so why hasn't she hit the tank yet? And if the truck burns, what happens to the samples she wants?" He shook his head. "We'd better sit tight."

Tisha's eyes were wide with fright. "Okay," she whispered.

There was another shot, then silence, as if Maria had heard their conversation.

The tension was almost unbearable. Zack worried about Tisha. Would she bear up? She was frightened, but her eyes continued to search her assigned field of view.

Time didn't exist anymore. Every second was the fullness of it. Where was she? What would she try next? The sun baked on.

Then there was the sound of a motor in the far distance. Had she left? But no, this was not a motorbike. This motor had a fuller, more powerful sound. And it was drawing closer, not farther away. It was coming fast.

Suddenly it was there. Zack heard the motor idle as the vehicle paused.

Then the air was shattered by the cracking, pounding percussion from a big gun. The fifty-caliber gun, Zack realized. He could see dust spurts and hear the thump of bullets as they stitched an arc across the road and into the surrounding desert, striking plants and rocks, digging trenches, perforating and destroying everything they touched.

CHAPTER THIRTY-FIVE

The big gun clattered to silence. There was only the idling motor sound of the DVP. Then Zack heard the chainsaw whine of a dirt bike undulating away into the distance. The buggy clutched into gear and drove close.

"You can come out now, White Man."

Zack stood on shaky legs and stared at the Navajo. Relief washed over him. He was alive, and his friend was as well. It was a good moment.

"It's about time you got here," he said.

"It took me a while to figure out the clutch," Eagle Feather said.

"You look a mess."

"You are not the picture of an FBI poster boy," Eagle Feather replied.

Zack was conscious of his sweat-soaked, dusty clothing. He picked up his hat from the ground and dusted it off.

"Where's Rackwell?" Eagle Feather asked.

Zack motioned toward the truck cab. "He's dead. Maria took him out to stop the truck."

Eagle Feather shook his head in regret.

"Shouldn't we get out of here?" Tisha asked, her voice edged in anxiety.

"Right," Zack said. "We'll have to leave Rackwell in the truck and let Janice take care of him." He turned to

Tisha. "Grab your rifle, your water, and anything else you need. I'll get the samples and the map."

The topo map was on the floor of the passenger seat. Zack picked it up after one last, regretful glance at Rackwell, the innocent, who had so unwittingly put himself in danger.

He walked to the DPV, where Eagle Feather waited.

"Now that you've learned to drive this thing," Zack said, "keep going. I'll navigate from this map."

Tisha reassumed her place at the fifty-caliber gun and began to thread a new ammunition belt into it.

Eagle Feather let in the clutch, and they stuttered off.

With the topo map flattened across his knees, he glanced between it and the surrounding landscape.

"Do you think she'll try again?" he asked Eagle Feather.

Eagle Feather nodded. "Yes. She has not completed her task."

"We'll make the next two lefts. That puts us on a road that will take us most of the way to the helipad.

Eagle Feather glanced at him. "Helipad?"

Zack grinned. "I've managed to talk Janice into another favor."

"How much gas is in this thing?" Eagle Feather asked. "Just curious."

"I guess we'll find out."

"Can you look at the map and guess where she'll hit us?"

Zack studied their route. "There are several places where the road narrows between cliffs. If we can get past those and onto the Randsburg Road, there are buildings and hopefully more people."

"That has never bothered her before," Eagle Feather said. "Our best chance is to outrun her. Give her no chance to prepare for us."

"We'll use more gas that way."

"One problem at a time," Eagle Feather said as he accelerated.

The road they were on was rough, but soon they reached the more traveled road, and the ride was a bit easier on their kidneys. They knew they could outdistance the dirt bike. But Maria had a slight head start.

They had descended a ridge into a flat desert basin between blue-tinged hills to the west and the rising Panamint Hills to the east. Despite his discomfort, Zack felt moved by the desolate beauty and grandeur of the place.

"My soul could get lost out here," he said.

"So could the rest of you," Eagle Feather replied.

They raced on, their dust elevating to great heights behind them. It was not a question of whether Maria could locate them. It was now a race for life.

"Look there!" It was a shout from Tisha in the gun seat.

Zack looked and saw she was pointing east, where an arroyo swept down the side of the mountain. A tiny plume of dust hung there.

"That's her," Zack said. "No one else would ride there. "She's behind us! She can't catch us now."

Eagle Feather crept the accelerator forward. They flew along the flatland.

"Do you think she can guess where we're going?" Tisha asked.

"Yes. Maria knew as soon as we turned south. We need to beat her there."

At that moment, the motor sputtered, caught again, and roared on.

No one said a word.

Zack held his breath, his full attention on the sound of the motor as if it was a ticking time bomb. After a time, he said, "Must have been dirt in the line."

No one replied.

The road ribboned beyond them to where it diffused into undulating heat waves at the edge of their view. Any relief from the airflow the speeding vehicle generated evaporated in the heat along with the moisture content of their skin. They passed a water bottle from one to another in a solemn ritual like wine at communion. Their coating of dust was like a second skin to them now.

Then the engine burbled, backfired, and quit. Eagle Feather pushed in the clutch, letting the DPV roll to a stop. He tried the starter. The engine cranked but did not fire.

Zack leaped out to look at the engine, sizzling and popping as it cooled. "This looks like a standard-size gas tank," he said. "It should hold maybe twelve gallons. Even with terrible mileage, we shouldn't be out of gas."

He glanced at Eagle Feather. The Navajo had retrieved his rifle and was checking its load and scope. He'd already moved on.

"Maybe it's an evaporative feed problem caused by the heat," Zack said hopefully. He peered at the fuel feed system. Every part of the motor looked incredibly dry.

When Zack looked down at the tank, a drop fell from it into the sand, disappearing as fast as it landed. A small piece of metal from the undercarriage had perforated the gas tank's metal wall. The leak came from a tiny crack.

Zack sighed and stood. "We were hit and never knew it," he said. "The tank has probably been leaking fuel ever since yesterday sometime. "We're not going anywhere."

He came back, sat down, and took out his phone. "It's time to call for a rescue."

"It had better be quick," Eagle Feather said.

Zack followed his gaze. In the distance behind them, a small dust cloud hovered. Maria was coming.

Zack called Janice

"Hello? Za..?"

That much was clear. After that, it was like speaking in a hollow chamber, Zack's voice rebounding over hers. They were experiencing sat lag.

Zack turned to look at the dust again. It was much closer. His frantic attempts to communicate with Janice only resulted in a gibberish of overlap with her voice.

In desperation, he yelled a single word:: "Help."

CHAPTER THIRTY-SIX

The dust plume behind them became truncated, wafted east in the air and dissipated. Maria was not close enough for them to see, and the effect was that she had disappeared.

"What's she up to?" Zack muttered.

"She knows we have stopped and is wondering why," Eagle Feather said.

Tisha had the fifty-caliber gun aimed that way. "Shall I give it a burst and see what she does?"

Zack shook his head. "I doubt she is in range, and she will not be intimidated. Best to save ammunition. I think we'll need it." His phone rang. "Thank God," he said, answering. "Hello, Janice?" At that moment, he noticed the phone announced, 'Incoming'.

"Hello?"

He heard a familiar, intoxicating voice. "Hello, Zack. I was sitting here wondering what you're up to, and then I thought, why not just give him a call and ask him?"

"How did you get this number?" Zack's wide-eyed glance conveyed to the others who had called.

Maria responded with a ripple of laughter. "Why, Zack, your silly little number was no problem for my army of hackers."

"What do you want?"

"You know what I want. All you have to do is leave the samples on your seat, and the three of you can walk away unharmed."

"We are three to your one and well-armed."

"You are sitting ducks, as they say."

Zack knew it was true. So long as they remained motionless in the lifeless vehicle, Maria could circle unseen, move into range, kill them one by one with a single shot, and be gone before the others could respond.

Zack tried a bluff. "You'll have to catch us first. We stopped to get a better satellite signal. We'll move on soon. Besides, we have a gunship coming. You barely survived your encounter with the last one. I suggest you give yourself up now."

Her laughter spilled out of the phone. "Oh, Zack, you are far too sincere by nature to lie. If I can hack your phone number, don't you think I can hear your conversations? Your helicopter will be waiting at the helipad, miles away. And I doubt it's a gunship." She giggled, then her voice turned cold. "I'll give you five minutes to walk away from your vehicle, leaving the samples behind. When the time expires, I'll shoot the girl first. I don't like her much."

The line went dead. Zack looked at the eyes on him.

"She wants us to walk away from the vehicle, leaving the samples. She says she'll spare us if we do."

"She is lying," Eagle Feather said without expression.

"I know," Zack said. "She gave us five minutes to decide."

DESOLATION

"Another lie. Maria is moving into position. She'll shoot when she acquires a target."

"But...but we have this big gun," Tisha said.

"You cannot shoot what you cannot see," Eagle Feather said.

"He's right. We won't know if Maria is in range until she kills one of us."

"But if we walk away, we become an even better target," Eagle Feather said.

Zack made his decision quickly. "We need to gather all the water we can, a trenching shovel, a long rifle for each of us, all the ammunition we can pocket, and crawl under this vehicle. We may have less than a minute." Zack moved even as he spoke.

Once under the vehicle, they hollowed out body positions and used that sand to build a wall beneath the buggy to limit Maria's view of them. Each took a compass point in a prone position with water at hand and extra ammunition at their feet.

"Well, this is cooler, anyway," Tisha said.

Zack took a position to cover the area to the west, Eagle Feather the east, and Tisha the north. Eagle Feather and Zack could swing toward the south if needed.

"It smells like gas under here," Tisha said. "Couldn't she just shoot the tank and blow us up?"

"That's unlikely with an empty tank, and in any event our sand wall makes it harder for her to see it. Once she

215

shoots, she'll have to move because we'll have a fix on her."

"She can simply wait us out," Eagle Feather said. "We can't stay here forever."

"We can move once it's dark," Zack said. He tried to sound optimistic.

"The sun is still high. We have hours to wait," Tisha said.

"It will be harder for her out there in the sun," Zack said. "Presumably, she has no shade."

"The heat will not bother her," Eagle Feather said. "Nothing does."

Silence fell among them with that, broken only by the sound of Tisha fidgeting in the sand. Zack waited, guessing she had more to say. Then it came.

"How did you two manage to piss off this killer robot so badly?"

"It's a long story," Zack said.

"The short version is, *he* did it," Eagle Feather said.

"I don't care, actually," Tisha said. "I just want this over."

A gusts of wind blew sand grains from his sand wall into Zack's face. He took his eye from the scope to wipe it away. When he looked back, he saw movement.

"I've got motion at twelve o'clock on my side," he said.

"Can you see her?" Tisha asked.

"Negative. Don't change position."

"How far away?" That was Eagle Feather.

"It's hard to tell...maybe a thousand yards."

"Well within her range," Eagle Feather said. "Yours also. Maybe try a shot at the location? Keep her honest?"

"Or kill a coyote," Zack said. He nestled the rifle snugly against his shoulder, set his aim, then waited. He sensed the tension around him. His view through the scope undulated with the heat vapor rising from the sand and rippling the surface of the desert into multiple planes.

With startling suddenness, something filled his scope lens. The image resolved into a wing followed by a red neck and beady eye. The vulture took flight.

Zack's tension shuddered away into limpness. "False alarm. It was a vulture."

"Keep looking," Eagle Feather said. "She might have disturbed it."

Zack kept his eye in the scope, but his mind leaped elsewhere. "Why do you suppose my phone's sat signal was so distorted with Janice yet so clear with Maria?" He didn't get an answer.

"What's that?" Eagle Feather said.

"What?"

"Listen."

They did.

"I don't hear anything," Tisha said.

217

Then Zack did hear it. It was the far off sound of an aircraft. As it neared, the sound became the familiar thwack-thwack of rotors.

"It's a helicopter," Zack said. His phone vibrated. He glanced at it. It was a message from Janice: "We're coming."

Zack read it aloud.

"Thank *God*," Tisha said.

"Maria might try to shoot them down," Eagle Feather said.

"Can't you ever be positive?" Tisha asked.

Zack grinned to himself. "Keep your watch until they've landed," he said.

They heard another sound beyond the approaching helicopter, the surging whine of a dirt bike.

"She's running," Eagle Feather said.

The pounding clamor of the helicopter sounded overhead, hovered momentarily, then thundered off. It made a wide circle and then returned. When it landed, the blowing sand struck the DPV like shrapnel.

Zack watched Janice step down, duck the blades, and walk toward them.

CHAPTER THIRTY-SEVEN

Janice walked across the desert sand like it was a day in the office, wearing black button-up boots, creased dark pants, a white blouse, and a black tailored jacket, her short black hair coifed in defiance of the wind. She appeared unarmed and vulnerable, but Zack knew of the Beretta holstered behind her back that she could use to deadly effect.

"Who is that?" Tisha asked in awe.

"That's my boss," Zack said, not without a touch of pride in his voice.

"She is a scary person," Eagle Feather said.

Janice halted near the desert buggy and stared down at them. "You can come out now."

Zack pushed away the sand before him and crawled out. He stood before her, sand covered, bedraggled, and painted with sweaty dust.

"I didn't think you'd gotten my message," he said.

"That pitiful call for help, you mean?" She gave a tight smile.

"We ran out of gas." Zack hung his head.

"One should always check one's fuel level before departing on a trip," Janice said.

"I know, I know."

She held Zack's eye. "Any wrecked vehicles to report?"

"No. Uh, maybe. Well, yes, but not ours."

"Any dead bodies to report?"

"Uh, well, yes, just one."

Janice sighed, then glanced at the approaching figures of Tisha and Eagle Feather. She gave a simple nod to the Navajo and stretched a hand out to Tisha.

"You must be Tisha Knolls from the Investigative Services Branch."

"Yes, ma'am." Tisha shook her hand.

"It's good to meet you," Janice said. "I've heard good things about you. We should work more closely with your well-trained group in the future."

Zack was becoming nervous. "We're rather exposed here, Janice. Maybe we should..."

"She's gone," Janice said. "She was disappearing into those hills over there as we approached. We gave your position a wide circle but found no heat signatures. We're alone."

She gave Zack a thoughtful look. "I may have to make room in my schedule to deal personally with Maria one day. It seems to me you might be letting her linger on." Her thoughtful look changed to a smile. "Well, grab your gear and come aboard. I'm sure this young lady would love a bite and a bath."

The helicopter was an FBI wonder, a technological aircraft fitted with every sound, sight, and sensing device imaginable. The interior glowed with blinking lights and bulged with monitors and computer banks. Janice and Tisha took the two comfortable seats aft of the pilot's compartment and left the two jump seats for Zack and Eagle Feather.

As they took off, Zack watched the infrared monitor screen displaying heat variations in the landscape they overflew.

Janice clicked into his earphones. "Tell me what you found," she said, swiveling her seat to face him.

"First, I found that Maria has hacked our phones. She sounded clearer on my phone than you did."

Janice did not show surprise. "I suspect that clarity is due to a different satellite."

Zack raised his brows. "You mean not one of ours."

"Precisely."

Zack digested that. It put a lot of things into perspective. A limited number of nations and corporations had the capability to launch or piggyback satellites into space.

"What did you find?" Janice asked again.

"We found something that looked like a meteor crater with a fused metal object at the center."

Janice looked thoughtful. "Where?"

Zack read the coordinates to Janice from his phone. She clicked away to another channel and spoke. Immediately the aircraft turned in a new direction.

She was back. "I've given the location to the pilot. We'll overfly it and see what we can learn from our instrumentation."

Zack watched other instrument panels come to life and realized someone forward in the copilot seat was operating them.

The landscape below showed in black and white but pulsed into various colors that seemed to illustrate land features in an ongoing cycle on one of the monitors.

Zack pointed. "What's that?"

"That's lidar," Janice said. "It uses pulsing lasers to measure distances to the earth. With it, we can see what lies beneath vegetation, buildings, and other obstructions."

Tisha broke into the conversation. "I saw that on an archeological documentary."

"I'm sure you did," Janice said. "Archaeologists use it extensively. We'll overfly the crater, take precise measurements and collect data and as we fly you back, the computers will analyze the data we collected."

"So you'll know all about it even before you land?" Tisha asked.

"Not all about it, but a lot. We'll take your samples to the lab. That will give us more answers."

"Can I go home now?" Zack asked.

"I'll still need you on the ground. There is something more going on here. I want you ready. All of you."

Eagle Feather's voice sounded. "By the way, there's a body you should pick up on the slope west of the crater."

"Whose body this time?"

"Someone who wanted to shoot us when we were taking samples from the object in the crater. Maria killed him."

"Another player?"

"Yes."

"We'll pick him up," Janice said.

The helicopter touched down near Tisha's truck twenty minutes later, and Janice left them there in a flurry of blowing dust.

The sun was low in the west as they piled in the truck. Eagle Feather decided to ride in the truck bed with his rifle.

Zack was surprised. "There's no way Maria could beat us back here on a dirt bike. Ride in the cab with us."

"We do not know if she is acting alone," the Navajo said.

Zack shrugged. He knew better than to argue.

It was dark by the time Tisha dropped them off at the resort. She refused the offer of a drink, pleading her need for a shower, food, and sleep. They agreed to meet for breakfast the following morning.

Zack and Eagle Feather ordered room service and took turns in the shower. They found beers in the mini-fridge and relaxed with them.

"When do you expect results from our samples?" Eagle Feather asked.

"We should get some preliminary information from Janice by tomorrow morning and hopefully the full results later in the day."

There was a knock at the door. Eagle Feather took a position against the wall while Zack answered. It was their meal on a cart. Zack rolled it into the room. The smell of burgers made Zack's stomach grumble.

"I wish you'd relax," Zack told Eagle Feather. "Maria is gone now. She failed. There's no reason for her to return."

Eagle Feather shrugged.

The meal was silent, their appetites voracious.

Dipping a fry into a pool of ketchup, Zack said. "If Barroff did bug the DPV, he must know where we went."

"But we didn't take it to the impact crater."

"True. If Barroff calls us to ask where the DPV is, we can assume he didn't bug the buggy."

Before Eagle Feather could answer, they heard a noise at the door. An envelope appeared beneath it.

"Now she's resorting to anthrax," Eagle Feather said.

Zack grinned but was wary. He put on a pair of plastic gloves and picked up the envelope. The address was to both of them.

Raising an eyebrow at Eagle Feather, Zack shook the envelope near his ear. Nothing rattled or moved. He peeled it open, unfolded the note, and read it.

"We are cordially invited to enjoy drinks at the Poolside Cafe with Billy Frank."

"When?"

"Right now."

CHAPTER THIRTY-EIGHT

Billy was waiting for them at the same table where he'd first approached Zack. He wore the same blanket and dust-smudged hat as before.

"You two morons move with all the speed of legless chickens," was his greeting.

"Good evening to you, too," Zack said, seating himself.

The old Indian raised three fingers. The barkeep grinned. Soon they heard the rhythmic tambourine of mixology.

"What did you order?" Zack asked.

Billy's good eye rolled toward him. "A James Bond drink for two bozo Bonds," he said. "What did you learn on your little trip?"

"It's above your pay level."

The old Indian cackled. "It's way above your intelligence level." He glanced from Eagle Feather to Zack. "So what landed on Wingate Pass and went boom?"

Zack's jaw dropped.

Eagle Feather gazed at the old Indian. "How far can your drone fly, Father?"

Billy slapped the table. "There! You see? Proper respect. Here's a man who knows how to respect his elders. White people do not know this simple courtesy."

Zack opened his mouth to respond but was interrupted by the arrival of their drinks. The barkeep placed them on the table and stood back, waiting.

Billy sampled his. His face grew thoughtful, then he grinned. "You found some Kina Lillet!"

The barkeep's boyish face beamed with delight. "Yes, sir, we just got some in."

Billy chuckled. "Forget what I told you yesterday. You can unpack your bags."

"Thank you, sir." The barkeep beamed a huge smile and bounced back to the bar.

"That boy tries harder than a constipated man in a timed pay toilet."

Zack narrowed his eyes. "Did you fly your drone to Wingate Pass?"

Billy snorted. "I watched you every foot of the way, moron."

Zack shook his head. "No way. It's too far for even the best non-military drones."

"Who says it was the same drone? We need to keep an eye on those asshole miners in the Panamints. We have a system, dumbass."

The impact of this revelation was overwhelming. "You know about the meteor crater."

Billy chuckled. "Try your drink while it's still cold."

Zack did. It was good.

Eagle Feather took up the question. "Why did you not tell us about it before we left?"

"I needed you morons to find it for me."

"How did you know about it?" Zack asked.

Billy wiped his nose on his sleeve. "We knew something had happened out there that night. We had a scheduled flyover the morning after the impact. It recorded minor damage at mine buildings; stuff knocked over, glass broken, that kind of thing. And we saw a bunch of people talking. Prospectors and miners aren't social people, so that was unusual."

"How'd you figure out what it was?"

"We knew it wasn't a mine explosion or a small earthquake because we checked the seismology for the area. There was nothing, not even a smothered fart. So we went to the sky and checked with a local amateur astronomy group. They'd been filming a time-lapse sequence that night, so we took a look. We saw this long streak of light come right out of the sky and into the hills. It had to be a meteor or the reentry of some space garbage. Something solid, though." He eyed Eagle Feather. "Yo! Navajo. Drink your drink, don't waste my money."

Eagle Feather ignored him and asked, "What is the purpose of this meeting?"

"Yeah, okay, no more foreplay. I wanna know what it was."

Zack stiffened. "This is an ongoing investigation. We can't—"

"Cut the bullshit. I'm talking tit for tat. I know stuff you need to know, and you know shit I need to know."

"What do you know?"

"Why people are trying to kill you, for a start."

"Okay, why?"

"You first."

"You have nothing."

Billy sighed. "I was hoping you were smarter than the average FBI dodo, but I'll spell it out. My people have one big concern. The earth. The land of our origins." He waved a hand in a southerly direction. "Those big companies mining for gold and other saleable metals are ruining it with arsenic, their huge pits, and the contaminated water runoff. Nobody's keeping an eye on them, so we got to. We got people with homes up there growing crops and raising goats and sheep like the old days, but when their water comes out of the ground full of arsenic, they can't survive. So we gave 'em a drone and taught 'em how to fly it and spy on those operations. It's all evidence for when we go to court and bring those companies down."

"Interesting, but not pertinent."

"Hold on to your panties, FBI. We don't just watch 'em from the air; we investigate them with the internet. Who are they, who owns them, what is their corporate structure, all that shit. We read their notes from board meetings, stockholder meetings, and shareholder reports. Everything. We know more about those bastards than they do about themselves."

"Impressive, but I still don't see a connection."

"I ain't got there yet. Some of the companies are shell companies owned by larger companies owned by even larger corporations, like those Russian dolls, one inside the other. But then there's Alset Corporation."

"Alset?"

"Used to be Borax."

"Borax? They're still in business?"

The eye leveled on Zack. "There ain't no twenty mule teams hauling wagons no more, dumb ass. And they don't work the mine here in the valley no more, either. It's just a museum. But that don't mean nobody's extracting boron around here."

"That's for washing hands and doing laundry," Zack said.

Billy snorted. "You need to go online and look up boron compounds. You got a lot to learn."

Eagle Feather was growing impatient. "What has boron got to do with this case?"

Billy scratched his armpit. "I ain't sure. I haven't figured that out yet. But one thing I do know, there's a lot of sudden interest in boron compounds."

"Are they mining it around Wingate Pass?" Zack asked. "Is that it?"

Billy shook his head. "Not there. Ever hear of a town with the name Boron?"

"South of here, down near California City?"

"Yeah, that's right."

"That's a long way from your people. What's your concern there?"

"We got interested 'cause we learned borates can be used instead of mercury amalgamation for extracting gold. We figured we could convince these local miners to use it instead of cyanide and mercury and all that shit."

"How'd that work out?"

"Not good. Not yet. But my point is, dumb ass, while lookin' into boron compounds, we found that shares in Rio Caca, the mining company there, were being snatched up real fast."

"Why?"

"Dunno."

"By who? Individuals? A group of people? A corporation?"

"By a country."

"What country?"

"China. And guess what, dorkweed, they now own fifty-four percent of the company stock."

CHAPTER THIRTY-NINE

Janice's lab report landed in his computer early the following morning. While more work lay ahead in the metallurgy lab, they identified the rock in the crater as a partial meteorite.

Zack called Janice. "What the heck is a partial meteorite?"

"The lab geeks say it is a composite of space and earth metals."

"How can earth metals come from space?"

"Well, that's the question, isn't it?"

"Did you learn anything from the lidar measurements?"

"The crater shape affirms a meteorite falling to earth. We have no doubt the alarming boom your late miner friend described was that event."

"Speaking of Brett, did you recover his body?"

"Yes, a team brought him out. They found a bullet fragment consistent with a high-power rifle." She gave a dry chuckle. "The lab has a shelf labeled probable Maria for all her bullet fragments. It went there. The team set the scene with the truck to look like a road accident. We'll have the local sheriff's office notify the next of kin and release the body to them."

"He was a good man. It's a shame."

"This is no time to be growing sentimental, Zack. We must consider you a target until we know more."

Zack shared the lab results with Tisha and Eagle Feather at breakfast in the resort dining room. He mentioned the warning from Janice.

Eagle Feather raised a questioning eyebrow. "The samples are now beyond Maria's reach, and word is out about the meteorite. She's finished. What else could keep her here?"

"I don't know," Zack said. "And that's the problem. We don't know enough yet."

"What was your conversation with Billy about?" Tisha asked.

Zack laughed. "I think we underestimated that old Indian yet again. He's got a whole eye-in-the-sky drone system set up. He followed us virtually our whole trip."

"He's keeping an eye on the mining concerns out there," Eagle Feather said. "He seemed to want to tell us that the Chinese own the lion's share of a boron mining company somewhere south of us."

They ate in thoughtful silence. The sun crystallized on the picture window, and its refracted light created a warm glow in the room.

Tisha set her fork down. "Why do you think Billy felt that particular information could be important to us?"

"Who knows? He's half nuts," Eagle Feather said.

"Whatever his thinking, it always comes down to the interests of his people," Zack said.

"And the land," Tisha added.

"True," Eagle Feather admitted.

As Zack's eyes wandered around the room, he noticed a young woman engaged in a phone conversation. It sparked a memory.

"Do you remember when I mentioned that Maria's call to me was somehow clearer than my satellite connection with Janice, even though Maria had hacked my number?"

They both nodded.

"And we thought she must have access to another satellite?"

"And you said only a large corporation or another nation would have the means to have launched a satellite," Tisha said.

"Right!"

She looked puzzled. "China? Do you think that's the China connection? That Maria might be working for China."

"Well, it's a possibility. Maria's services as an elite assassin are expensive and in global demand. So why not?"

"Let me get this straight," Tisha said. She ticked the facts on her fingers. "We know China owns a controlling interest in a company mining boron nearby. China sends Maria to intercept Sweiger, who is searching for something near Wingate Pass. The Navy hires Eagle Feather to find out what happened to Sweiger. Soon after, Maria attempts to kill Eagle Feather. Then, Maria attempts to kill us when we meet with Commander Barroff, and failing that, she follows us to Wingate Pass to try to stop us. Right so far?"

Both men nodded.

"But then it falls apart. Maria visits us at Rackwell's mine to tell us her orders have changed, and she no longer plans to kill us. Plus, now there's someone else out there trying to kill us."

"She lies a lot," Eagle Feather said.

"But there *was* someone else trying to kill us or at least keeping an eye on us," Zack pointed out.

"Her purpose was to set us up so we would lead her to the meteorite crater. She knew her adversary would follow us there," Eagle Feather said.

"Killing two birds with one stone," Tisha breathed.

"One, at least. And Maria did her best to ambush us and steal our samples," Zack said. "She killed Rackwell, so yes, she did lie."

"But she failed to get the samples," Eagle Feather said.

Tisha gave a triumphant look. "Exactly. It *does* work. Billy gave us the final dots. The connected dots bring China, Maria, and the meteorite together."

"What about Sweiger?" Zack asked. "Where's his dot?"

"Who sent him? Who did he work for, you mean?" Tisha asked.

"Right. It couldn't be the home team. If the U.S. wanted to get to the meteorite site, they'd send a helicopter to search. There'd have been Marines swarming all over the pass."

"True. But who else could it be?"

Zack stared into his water glass. "And after all, what's the motive? What's so important about the meteorite? For that matter, who cares if China owns a controlling interest in a company mining boron? People have mined it for various purposes for centuries." He shook his head. "We're missing a big piece here."

"So what's our next act, Shakespeare?" Tisha said with a teasing grin.

"I'd like to pay another visit to Esther Flores," Zack said. "I'd like to know why she sent us off to the Panamint Mountains in the first place."

CHAPTER FORTY

"White folks are not in touch with their spiritual sensitivities," Esther said. "There are more ways to see the world than with your eyes. A blind person can understand what she hears, smells, and touches better than one who can see. It must be so for her to navigate her world."

She paused to sip her tea.

Zack sat across the table from her, breathing the relaxing aroma of a tincture of *Lavandula Angustifolia* brewed in *Camellia Sinensis* that wafted up from his cup.

"My Navajo friend has told me so many times," he said.

She nodded. "Yet it is not exclusively cultural, but a cultivated consciousness. We choose how and where to direct our focus. Increasingly, in the modern world, people focus on personal comfort, power, and immediacy, for which we require communication devices, tangible possessions, and media. One must remain absorbed in such pursuits 24/7 to succeed in such a world, leaving no time to develop other realities."

"So you're saying, put down the iPad and try to sense the other worlds around you."

Esther smiled. "The other worlds *in* and around you, yes. But Native Americans have had centuries of experience in such awareness. I wouldn't suggest abandoning the material world cold turkey; reserve some time to explore other worlds."

Zack sipped his tea. Its warmth and relaxing sensation flowered inside him, absorbing his tension like a sponge.

He set his cup in its saucer. "When last we met, you spoke of caves, legends, and mysteries in the Panamint Mountains. Your words prompted us to go there. Had we not gone, we would not have found evidence important to our investigation. Did you know this would be true?"

She thought for a few moments. "I felt a sense of connectivity between you and those mountains. No more than that. But my sense of such synchronicity is seldom wrong, although the connection may always be clear."

"Carl Jung?"

"Among others. Jung defined such connections in analytical terms. For me, it is not so complicated."

"Where does that sense come from?"

"Everywhere. All around me, there is spiritual connectedness. My people have always known it."

"Perhaps the Wingate Pass suggestion came in part from your brother," Zack suggested.

Esther smiled. "The cynic in you emerges. How does Eagle Feather deal with that?"

"He ignores it."

"Well, I won't. I indeed share my brother's interest in preserving our land from the depredations of miners and greedy corporations, but our methods are wildly different. He is hands-on with his technology and spies, while I am the queen of quiet protest, appealing to hearts and minds."

Zack laughed. "I sense a toughness in you beyond that description. But my point is, could your intuitive sense connecting me to the Panamints have come from some conversation with your brother?"

"I could protest all I want, of course, for a cynic is a cynic always. However, your focus, if I may point it out, is on your narrow agenda, that of solving your crime. My agenda is toward a wider purpose, saving our land. My spiritual sense, or as you put it, my intuition, told me that good would come from directing your attention to those hills, benefiting both of us."

"How might it benefit your purposes?" Zack asked.

"I believe that is yet to come."

"May I ask why your people have historically clung to this desolate land?"

"I am glad you ask that question. I have two answers for you. The first is simple. Desolation is a matter of perspective. I consider an empty city street at night the essence of desolation. We, the Timbisha Shoshone have lived the way we do here in the valley from first memory. It is our way of life, and it fulfills us. We had all we needed to be happy until people came here to extract minerals, take the water, move our villages, and claim the land for themselves. One becomes accustomed to one's day-to-day life and resists changing it."

She didn't wait for Zack to respond.

"My second answer is a metaphor. Consider the mesquite tree. It is well-adapted to this land, with its long, thin needlepoint leaves. It sustains itself with the water that lies far beneath the surface. Its taproot can reach lengths of a hundred and ninety feet. If calamity strikes, the mesquite can regenerate from one small piece of root in the soil. Its new growth begins with long, protective thorns, defensive from birth. The tree enjoys the alkaline soils where other plants would die."

"The Mesquite is well adapted to its environment, is your point," Zack said.

"But there is more. It communes, shares, and gives back. It provides shade where no other trees can live. It grows a tiny flower that attracts many pollinators. It grows seed pods that feed animals and humans. My people traditionally grind the seed pods into flour to make our cakes. You call this relationship among living things symbiosis. For us, it is more. It is the spiritual connectedness of living things. We are spiritually connected to our land."

Her eyes searched Zack's face. "Would you wish to be taken from your family?"

Zack shook his head. "No, of course not. Yet, it can be easy to become accustomed to modern comforts."

Esther smiled. "Is it not true that those comforts are available in direct relationship to wealth and power? Some have more comforts than others. Traditionally, my people have shared the same comforts and discomforts alike."

"Yet your brother has adapted well to modern times."

"My brother has an anger inside him that stems from the ill-treatment our people received. He uses techniques and processes from your world to gain power against your intrusions and greed. But it has not made him a happy man."

"I hope we can continue our relationship and further our separate agendas," Zack said. "Your brother has been helpful in that regard."

"It serves his purposes as well. But what do you think I can do for you?"

Zack gave himself time to structure his thoughts with another sip of tea. The cool, silent interior of Esther's home was relaxing.

"You have your finger on the pulse of this valley. In your efforts to protect the land, you have learned what people want here and how they attempt to attain it. Historically over the centuries, it has been gold, silver, antimony, copper, lead, zinc, tungsten, boron, talc, fluorspar, cinnabar, Epsom salts, mercury, sodium chloride, manganese—what am I missing?"

"Uranium."

"Ah. But aren't all of these metals essentially mined out?"

"No. Gold, boron, and talc have made miners wealthy in the past, and mines still produce those elements in some areas. There are no active mines within the national park boundaries anymore, but there are working mines in all the surrounding hills. What they do there affects us here. But the cost of extracting minerals can be prohibitive when the market is down."

"But when the market is back up, it becomes feasible."

"Exactly."

"There seems to be an increasing interest in boron. Have you noticed that?"

Esther's eyes flashed to Zack's face. "I have."

"Why is that?'

"I don't know, but I do know that a Chinese state-controlled company has been buying into boron mining companies throughout the region."

"But you don't know why."

"No."

"Is it uncommon for a company from another nation to operate here?"

"Not at all. It's a natural progression. Most of the ores found here are expensive to extract, and as we discussed before, it's not worth the bother until the market is right. The smaller, local companies can't afford to wait, so they make their money selling out to a larger company that can. Those huge, global corporations can wait as long as it takes."

CHAPTER FORTY-ONE

"Our analysis of the samples from your meteorite is confusing, to say the least," Janice said. "The lab found aluminum alloy 6061, titanium, boron, beryllium, carbon, and a whole bunch of trace metals. The geeks think the aluminum and much of the carbon is earth-based, while the other metals, particularly the boron, and beryllium, are of a pure form not found naturally on Earth."

Zack caught the mention of boron. "How much of the boron was present in the samples?"

"Somewhere between forty-five and sixty percent, if I remember."

"And the purity of the boron?"

"Extraordinary."

"But the aluminum had to be from Earth."

"Right."

"So it had to be a chunk of some kind of space vehicle, like a rocket, satellite, or something like that?"

"That's what the lab thinks."

"What does all this tell you?" Zack asked.

"I haven't the foggiest idea," Janice admitted. "But I plan to run it up the flagpole to the scientific community to see if this corresponds to any new research."

"We suspect China has a role in whatever is going on," Zack said. "Just what, we don't know, but it seems boron is involved. Mention that to the scientific guys, will you?"

"And Maria?"

"She is linked to the whole China boron piece. My best guess is she works for China to protect their interests, which seem to have something to do with the boron. She very much wanted those samples we took away from the meteorite."

"She failed in that. Will she go away now?"

"Maybe. When this started, Maria tried to prevent anyone from getting to the meteor site, starting with Sweiger. Then she tried to stop us from reaching the impact area. But when we got close, Maria practically invited us to go there. She knew someone else was involved, so she set him up using us as bait, then killed him. What did you learn from that man's body?"

Janice hesitated. "There was nobody, Zack. Our people were all over the area before my bird had even landed, but there was no body."

Zack digested that for a moment. "So, whoever that killer worked for got there pretty damn quick."

"So it would seem."

"Who would have the resources to do that?"

"I can think of a few."

Zack was frustrated by her answer. "Okay, Janice, it's in your hands now. My work is complete. There's nothing left to investigate now."

Fatigue had begun to make slow inroads into Zack's mind and body. The thought of home and rest loomed large.

Janice's voice was soft. "Zack, I hate to say this. You've been through a lot—all of you—but I'd like you to stay on until all the answers to my inquiries are in." She paused. "I just have a feeling about this thing."

Zack laughed. "*You* have a feeling. That's funny. It's usually the other way around."

Her retort was in her normal voice. "Maybe it feels like you haven't destroyed enough FBI vehicles yet. Give me another forty-eight hours." She ended the call.

Zack turned to Eagle Feather with a wry grin. "I've got good news and bad news. The bad news is Janice wants us to stay for another few days. The good news is, I have carte blanche to destroy another vehicle."

Eagle Feather listened without comment. "Tisha's boss called her back to her office. She told me while you were with Esther."

The two friends had been enjoying a beer in their room when Janice called, Zack reclining on the bed, and Eagle Feather relaxing in a chair.

"I figured it would be soon," Zack said. "We'll have to give her a proper send-off at the pool bar."

Eagle Feather nodded. He thought for a moment. "Why does Janice want us to stay?"

"She just wants us handy. She wants the whole business wrapped up in a nice pink ribbon before releasing us."

"There is no pretty way to wrap this up. But, there are worse places to be." Eagle Feather sipped his beer.

There was a knock on the door. Eagle Feather went to open it. Tisha came into the room.

"I came to say goodbye," she said.

"We were just discussing your departure," Zack said. "It felt like it needed more than a simple adios after what we've been through."

Tisha smiled, and her blue eyes flashed. "I've got some time. What did you have in mind?"

Zack suggested the poolside celebration, and Tisha enthusiastically agreed. The three companions walked down the corridor toward the elevator making small talk. They felt like siblings who had known one another their entire lives, with nothing new left to say.

They rode the elevator in silence. When they stepped into the lobby, Tisha said, "This feels more like a wake than a celebration."

"I feel the same way," Zack said. "Maybe it's because this doesn't feel like the usual end to an investigation. There are too many loose ends."

"Right," Tisha said. "I still don't know what was going on. People died, but we still don't know why."

"I suppose the answers are above our pay grades," Zack said.

Tisha's eyes flashed. "Well, I don't like that. When I put my life on the line, I want to know why."

"It is good you don't work for the FBI, then," Zack said. "You would spend most of your time frustrated."

They stepped out onto the patio walkway. It was early evening, the sun low on the horizon, its remaining heat filtered by the shade of palms. To Zack, it felt like Nirvana after their hot, dusty desert experience. He remembered Tisha mentioning her preference for outdoor picnic lunches when they first met. He understood that now.

He had a call from Janice just as they entered the pool area. Zack motioned to Tisha and Eagle Feather to go ahead.

"The other shoe just dropped," Janice said.

"Meaning?"

"The meteorite samples have disappeared."

CHAPTER FORTY-TWO

"Wait! What? I thought they were in the lab. Your tech guys analyzed them. You have their reports."

"They called me just now. The samples are gone."

Zack was flabbergasted. "Isn't that lab one of the most secure places anywhere?"

"It wasn't a break-in," Janice said. "At least, not the physical kind. When I made inquiries, they told me to stand down."

"But...but you have the data from the analysis."

"Without the actual evidence, it is useless."

"Wait a minute. I know you, Janice. You didn't call me only to tell me our boat is sinking. You have a plan. What is it?"

"Nothing, officially. The FBI is no longer involved. However, you have some vacation time coming. I want you to enjoy a few days more in that nice resort."

"Janice, thanks, but...oh!" The light dawned. "And what will you be doing?"

"It so happens I already put in a call to a friend regarding satellites and related research. He promised to poke around. I'm just going to answer his return call when it comes."

"Got it!"

"But Zack, be careful. There is a cover-up, and they might start tying up some loose ends. The three of you could be one of them."

Zack pocketed his phone. His head brimmed with the news. The specimens were gone, hijacked from the lab by people with enough power to do such a thing to the FBI. Their investigation had halted. Then there was the warning from Janet and her helplessness. This sort of thing never happens, yet it just did.

Zack instinctively moved his left bicep against his ribs, feeling for the Sig Sauer he usually carried, then remembered he was wearing just a short-sleeve shirt and had left the weapon in his room. Tisha would not be armed, and Eagle Feather never carried a gun except in the field. He swallowed, his throat suddenly dry. Janet would never issue such a specific warning over the phone unless she felt the danger was imminent.

He stepped into the pool area.

The disappearing sun was throwing its last brilliant colors against the sky, mirrored in the pool. A slight breeze danced among the tall palms, setting their fronds swaying gracefully. The tented bar kiosk by the pool glowed with tiny bright lights. People were seated at tables, their conversations low as if hushed by the magical transference from day to evening occurring around them.

Eagle Feather and Tisha were at a poolside table. The setting sun color palette sparkling across them as the pool waters rippled with the moving night air. And then Zack saw her.

She sat three tables away, a solitary figure, blending so well into the ambiance that Zack almost missed her, would have, had she not caught his eye and then looked away. She was a woman tonight, her elegant facial features visible even at this distance, her slender form in a cocktail dress cut just low enough with embroidered lace at the bosom and oh-so narrow at the waist. Her lustrous dark hair cascaded onto her bare shoulders, glistening with the moving light as she turned her head away. Zack was too far away to peer into the dark depths of her eyes but felt their intensity.

Once again, the strange, primal feeling swept over him that if he must die, let it be by the hand of this unearthly, incredibly beautiful being with the power to seduce him even at a distance.

He was not alone. The heads of men at nearby tables, even those with families, turned to send glances her way.

To reach his friends, Zack must pass by her table. Had Eagle Feather seen her? He must have, yet his face showed his customary calm. He did not look at Zack.

Then Tisha spotted him and waved, half rising from her feet to catch his attention. Of course, she would not have noticed the beautiful assassin. Tisha had seen her just once, in a different setting, playing a different role.

Zack gave a small, half-hearted wave of his hand in response, his mind struggling to decide his next move. He should turn and walk away, he knew. He could not face Maria without a weapon, without a chance. She would not hesitate to kill all three of them right here and now, with barely audible spits from her silenced pistol, then glide swiftly and gracefully away. All the men would watch her seductive figure and not notice the inert forms at the table.

But for Zack to walk away now was to delay the inevitable. He would return armed only to find her seated at their table, with Tisha and Eagle Feather as her hostages, but then give up his weapon anyway in the slim hope that would save their lives, and they would die anyway.

As he stood there, still smiling awkwardly at Tisha, another familiar face turned toward him, then away. He recognized the scarred-faced old Timbisha, Billy Frank, sitting at his usual table. Would Billy know what was happening? Zack doubted it. And even if he did, there was little he could do.

What bothered Zack most, perhaps even beyond the prospect of death and the devastation that would bring to the lives of Libby and his precious son, was the thought that even after listening to the warning from Janice, he'd left the room without his gun. It was a careless, thoughtless act that would likely be his last.

There was just one course of action left, to Zack's mind. He walked into the cafe, past Tisha and Eagle Feather, directly to Maria's table, and sat down.

She smiled at him like a child receiving her most desired gift under the tree on Christmas morning.

"How wonderful of you!" she said, speaking in the low and slightly husky voice Zack found at once alarming and exciting. "You haven't a subtle bone in your body, have you?"

Maria had never appeared so enchanting as at that moment. Her dark eyes sparkled and glistened. She radiated her delight with energy almost unfathomable.

Zack lowered his head numbly. "You left me no choice."

Her laughter trilled, spreading infectiously to nearby tables where smiles appeared at the sound.

"Oh, dear Zack, there's always a choice." She held his eye with a fond look onlookers saw as a lover long parted and now reunited. She giggled. "But this was the best one, truly the best!"

Zack lifted his head. "There's no reason—"

She quieted him with a hand over his on the table. It was ice cold. "Didn't we have fun? That whole wonderful chase through the desert hills? The near misses, the bait and switch? Admit it, Zack, that was clever of me. Then the standoff at the truck! Zack, if you'd given me those samples, I would have let you live!" She pouted. "Just you, though. I didn't like that blonde bitch hanging on you."

Her frown vanished as fast as it had appeared, replaced by a childlike excitement. "Then your Navajo friend riding to the rescue with that big gun! Boom, boom, boom, boom! It was awesome! He does have nine lives, doesn't he?"

Suddenly her animated face blanked, and the life in her eyes died and became vacant, her attention caught by something beyond Zack. She was making a peremptory motion with her hand as one would signal a dog to sit.

Zack glanced there and saw Eagle Feather, half risen from his seat, inch back into it. The moment lasted seconds, and the sparkle returned to Maria's eyes.

She wagged a finger at Zack. "You and your helicopters. You almost killed me twice! As I said, you are not a subtle person."

Zack did not respond.

She studied his face. "You left your Sig Sauer in the room, didn't you?"

The question was rhetorical.

"Did you think the game was over?" She giggled again. "The Queen is still on the board." She wagged a finger. "Never mind what happens to the King; it's the Queen you need to watch."

"I guess I—"

"Go sit with your friends." Her eyes went beyond him, her face cold again. She was a child whose patience had run out.

Zack stumbled to his feet, turned and bumbled to the empty chair next to Tisha and Eagle Feather, and sat, his back to Maria.

Tisha's eyes were round with wonder. "What's going on?" she whispered.

"Do either of you have a weapon?" Zack asked.

"Just my knife," Eagle Feather said.

"On your right or left side?" Zack asked.

"Left."

Zack moved six inches closer to Tisha, opening a space toward Maria's table for Eagle Feather. He whispered to Tisha. "Keep an eye on the woman I was just with. When she reaches a hand toward her body, get down."

"Is it her? Maria?" Her voice sounded subdued.

"Yes."

With the corner of his eye, Zack caught movement at the bar. The young barkeep stepped from behind it holding a tray above his head. He threaded among the tables, moving toward them.

Zack saw Eagle Feather grow tense and his left hand creep down. Tisha's eyes were even rounder, if possible. Zack turned his head to look.

CHAPTER FORTY-THREE

There was an order to what happened next, but it seemed one blur of motion.

The bartender dropped his tray with a tremendous din of breaking glass and gonging metal. The people at the nearest tables jumped up and pressed their bodies away from flying glass and liquid, uttering sounds of dismay.

The bartender, unaffected, turned toward Billy Frank and pointed at him, and Zack then realized the hand held a gun, and the "pfft" sound of a silencer came, and the old Timbisha slumped in his chair.

Next to Zack, Tisha was ducking. Something whistled past Zack's ear, and he saw Maria forced backward by the knife in her left shoulder, but her right hand rose above the table, and in it was a silenced pistol.

Eagle Feather came crashing to his feet, but Zack sat immobile, staring as Maria's pistol continued its methodical rise.

The bartender had turned back toward them now, his arm coming around, his silenced gun swinging their way.

Maria's pistol was now at shoulder height. Zack stared with macabre fascination into the small, dark cavity of the silencer from where the bullet marking his end would fly, the one he would never see.

But the pistol barrel kept moving on its upward sweep, then away from him. Zack's eyes followed it to where it stopped, and beyond it, he saw the waiter's gun pointed directly at him.

The two silenced shots seemed simultaneous, but they were not. Something impacted Zack's table with a jolt. The bartender's gun drooped and then fell. A look of surprise came to his face, along with a hole in his forehead, then he collapsed to his knees, teetered, then dropped to the ground, dead.

Eagle Feather was rushing toward Maria's table, but she was no longer there. She was among the customers near the dead bartender. Zack heard her crying, "Oh, please help him. Something has happened to him."

People were standing, obscuring the crouching Maria from view. Zack found his feet finally and moved toward them. But when he got there, she was gone.

Then he realized they should not linger. He grabbed Eagle Feather by the arm.

"Get Tisha. We'll meet in my room."

Eagle Feather nodded and dissolved through the crowd.

Zack walked to Billy's table. No one had noticed the old Indian slumped in his chair, apparently dozing over his drink. His shirt bloomed with seeping blood around his heart.

Zack put his hand over the still hand of the old Timbisha. "Rest in peace, old friend," he said. "Your people will sing of your deeds."

Then he slipped away.

When Zack came to his room, he found the door unresponsive to his key. He knocked and announced himself in a whisper. His phone vibrated in his pocket. The message read, "Reply to this message."

He did, and the door opened, and he slid in. It was completely dark until the door closed behind him. Then a light came on. He saw the blinds drawn.

"We can't stay here," Eagle Feather said.

"I know. Pack what you need. Let's go."

"Where?" Tisha asked.

"I know someone who can help us," Zack said.

"Who was that man who tried to kill us?" Tisha asked.

"Questions have to wait," Zack said. "We need to get to safer ground. Now."

Everything Zack needed went into a backpack or his courier case. He left his suitcase, night clothes, and personal items in the room. "Let them believe I'm still here," he said.

They slipped out by the rear exit stairs.

"They'll be watching the truck," Eagle Feather said.

"We'll take the rental Tisha provided. I never used it," Zack said. He looked a question at her. She led the way to a red Toyota hatchback at the rear of the lot.

Zack produced the key from his pocket and unlocked it. Tisha took the passenger seat, and Eagle Feather climbed in the rear with the backpack and courier case. Zack took the wheel. The little car started, and they drove out of the lot.

As they passed the front of the resort, they saw flashing red and blue lights reflecting onto the building exterior and bright yellow lights back at the pool area.

"Just in time," Zack breathed.

"You now have one last chance, White Man," Eagle Feather said.

"For what?"

"To wreck another rental vehicle."

"Not so funny," Zack said.

"Where are we going?" Tisha asked.

"To see Esther Flores," Zack said. "She needs to know about her brother."

"Oh. Do I need to go get my things?"

"Not just yet. We need to wait and see."

They rode in silence after that.

It was fully dark but for a slight glow above the far western mountains, and the headlights of the little car slashed into the blackness before them.

The Timbisha village appeared as a twinkle of lights in the distance, then spread and became individual window lights of homes as they neared. Esther's house was dark but for a single half-shaded window.

Zack walked alone to the front door and knocked. After a moment, the porch light came on, and in another moment, the door opened to reveal Esther in a robe and slippers.

She appeared serene as she welcomed him, almost as if she had expected him.

"It is late. You bring news. Please come in."

"My friends are in the car."

"They are welcome, too."

Zack turned and waved. The car doors opened.

Zack stepped into the foyer.

"I do bring news," he said. "Sad news."

"It is my brother, isn't it?"

Before Zack could reply, Eagle Feather and Tisha were with them.

"Come in, all of you," she said. "She closed the door behind them and ushered them toward the sitting room.

Zack stepped to the window and lowered the blind.

"Do you mind? No one should know we are here for now."

Esther nodded, her expression unchanging. Zack wondered how much of what he must say she intuitively already knew."

"Please sit, Esther."

When she did, he pulled a chair close and took her hand. "I must tell you that your brother is dead," he said.

"I know this," was her reply. "Billy's spirit came to me." Her face showed the serenity he had noticed before. "How did it happen?"

"The waiter at the bar shot him and attempted to shoot us," Zack said. "We know now he was more than a barkeep, but we know nothing else."

Her eyes went to each of them and settled on Eagle Feather. She waited.

"Oh, I'm sorry," Zack said. "This is my friend Eagle Feather."

The Navajo nodded gravely. "There is sadness in my heart for your loss."

"You are Navajo," she said.

"I am."

"You are welcome." She turned to Zack. "You seek a place to hide. You will stay here."

Zack stood. "No. We will not bring danger to your home. We have caused enough sadness."

Her smile was sad. "Someone would have killed my brother even if you had never come here. I have always known this. Billy was like the woodpecker on a tree to the power establishment, always probing and picking at them to find their secrets."

Tisha raised her brows. "Who do you think wanted to kill him?"

"Too many to name," she said. "The mining interests, the Chinese, the government—"

"The government?" Zack asked. "What is their involvement?"

Her kind expression turned grim. "The government regards my people as aliens always ready to undermine the

260

United States. The Timbisha Shoshone people have always been problematic to the park service and the people who govern it. We refused to leave our homeland, the land they wished to set aside to allow people to come and stare like visitors in a zoo. But we refused to leave, and we continue to fight for our homeland."

She wiped an eye where perhaps a tear had lodged. "I am an activist in their eyes because of my words, but my brother was a revolutionist to them because of his actions. The government would not turn the other cheek to him, and that is why government agents have come here."

"Perhaps," Zack said. "But I think government interests extend toward something more complex than your brother's actions, or your people, for that matter."

Esther smiled through her tears. "Let me fix you some tea," she said.

261

CHAPTER FORTY-FOUR

While Esther bustled about in the kitchen, Zack called Janice.

"I've got news for you," Janice said.

"And I have news for you." Zack went on without waiting for her response. "The bartender shot and killed Billy Frank, then tried to shoot me, but Maria killed him first, while Eagle Feather tried to kill her with his knife but only wounded her."

There was a long silence.

"Where did all this happen, at the OK Corral?"

"At the Poolside Cafe, actually."

"And Maria?"

"Disappeared, as usual."

"Who was this bartender?"

"We don't know. We needed to get out of there, not knowing if the barkeep had allies. We left the hotel and are at a safe location, but we need you to sort this out so we know who is gunning for us."

"Did local law respond to the scene?"

"Yes. We saw the flashing lights as we drove away."

"Okay. I'm scrambling your phone signals so no one can locate you. Tell Tisha to remove her phone battery. Stay where you are until I get back to you."

She ended the call.

Tisha had been listening to Zack's conversation with rapt attention. Zack passed on Janice's message.

"What will happen now?" Tisha asked.

"I don't know. Janice wants us to remain here until further notice."

"It is interesting that Maria killed the man intending to kill us," Eagle Feather remarked.

"It begs the question of whether she was there to kill us or kill him," Zack said.

"Or both?" Tisha asked. She shivered. "I've never felt so vulnerable."

Zack patted his belt holster. "At least we're armed now. It was a rookie mistake to leave my gun in the room."

Esther padded back in with a tray that held four steaming cups and saucers. "My magic tea," she announced. "It will make us all feel better."

=

Janice called back around midnight. Zack was still up, although Eagle Feather and Tisha were asleep in the guest bedrooms Esther had offered.

"I've contacted the Sheriff's Department," Janice said. "No witnesses mentioned any of you in particular. Their attention had been on the bartender and Maria. Local homicide officers are looking into the credentials

263

of the barkeep from the resort files, but they are undoubtedly false. The dead barkeep is a ghost. We offered to run facial recognition software through every file containing known or suspected agents, domestic and foreign. It could be days before we have a match, if at all. And, of course, there is no sign of Maria, nor could anyone at the scene describe her well. Of course, we have our own file on her, but I thought it best not to share."

"What do we do in the meantime?" Zack asked.

" I have some news but want to meet you in person to deliver it."

"Will the mountain come to Mohamed, then?"

"This time, yes. Can we meet where you are now?"

"Yes, I think so."

"I'll call you on my secure line when I get to Furnace Creek. You can give me directions then."

When Zack put his phone down this time, he felt safe enough to fall fast asleep.

When he awoke, Zack found the others already up. Eagle Feather had been up early, conversing with Esther in low tones. Tisha had awakened early enough to help Esther make breakfast, and Zack rose in time to eat it with them.

All three guests enjoyed the peace and stillness in Esther's snug home, tucked away from any likelihood of disturbance. But the sadness of loss hung over the meal, despite Esther's attempts to banish it.

Janice called at eleven from Furnace Creek airport. She had arranged for a car and was on her way after receiving directions. Twenty minutes later, a knock sounded on the front door.

Zack was surprised to see Janice accompanied by another agent. She introduced him as Special Agent Thomas Heard from the Operational Technology Division of the FBI.

Heard was small and wiry, with a tufted mustache and balding head, giving an overall impression of a terrier. He shook hands all around.

"Agent Heard is here at my request," Janice began. "I've asked him to help explain some of what we've learned about this case."

She turned to Esther. "Please accept my deepest condolences on the loss of your brother. Do feel free to sit in on this meeting. You certainly deserve to know what happened."

Esther went to brew more tea as everyone found seats.

"I'm going to let Agent Heard begin with a technical overview." Janice nodded to him.

Heard looked at his open palms as if they could help him decide how to begin. Then he looked up.

"You all know Silicon Valley and how it gained its nickname from the material's unique properties as a semiconductor, which made the development of small electronic devices possible. Silicones protect against heat, shock, and contaminants. But suppose there was another compound that could potentially conduct heat up to ten times faster than silicon?"

"They'd have to rename the valley," Zack said.

"Exactly! Everyone producing small electronic devices would line up to acquire the stuff. And that, in a nutshell, is what we're dealing with here."

"Is there such?" Tisha asked.

"Maybe," Heard said. "And that's a qualified maybe. The material is cubic boron arsenide. Theoretical predictions of its properties were made in 2018 by a professor at MIT. Later research has demonstrated it provides high mobility to both electrons and holes and has excellent thermal conductivity. They say it is the best semiconductor material ever found, maybe even the best possible."

"Thomas, let's not get too technical with the electrons and holes and stuff," Janice said.

"Uh, sure. Sorry." He went on. "As you can imagine, researchers got excited about the possibilities. The U.S. Office of Naval Research threw its financial support behind the work. But up to now, cubic boron arsenide has only been made and tested in small, lab-scale batches that are not uniform." Heard raised empty palms. "Here's the question. Can the material ever be produced in a practical, economical form, with enough stability to replace good old silicon?"

"Can it?" Zack asked.

Heard smiled. "Eventually, we can do anything. Someone will hit on a way. The problem stalling everyone now is the inclusion of impurities occurring during production. Research continues, with tech companies eyeing each other carefully for a breakthrough. As you can imagine, the discoverer can name his price."

"What does this all have to do with our case?" Tisha asked.

"It's my turn now," said Janice, nodding to Heard. "There are several corporations and countries with great interest in this research. Two, in particular, have taken action in a most practical way. The first is a global corporation called Alset Industries, which produces everything from phones to electric vehicles. The other is China. The reasoning they both adopted was when, and if, there is a breakthrough with cubic boron arsenide, they needed to own a monopoly on the raw materials required."

"Boron and arsenic," Tisha breathed.

"Exactly. So each set about acquiring all the boron it could locate. Arsenic is prolific on the planet, but boron, not so much. For example, the world's second-largest metals and mining corporation now owns Twenty Mule Team Borax, and a Chinese state-owned enterprise is its largest shareholder. Both Alset Industries and China are buying up the limited places on earth where boron is found, like here in the southwest deserts of the U.S.A. and Turkey."

"That's not illegal," Zack said.

"Not at all. But here's what happened next." Janice turned to Heard.

CHAPTER FORTY-FIVE

Special Agent Thomas Heard took the ball back from Janice without a hitch and addressed the group like a professor in a lecture hall.

"Does anyone here know where boron comes from?"

"The Earth," Tisha said.

"Space," Zack said.

Heard smiled. "You are both right, in a way. Boron is the result of a collision between cosmic rays and space dust. Cosmic rays are nuclei traveling at super high speed, and when they strike an atom, they break it apart to form new elements. It happens all the time in space. Boron and beryllium form this way. Rain brings those elements down to the ground when spallation occurs in our atmosphere. So you see, you are both right."

Heard smiled at them as if at two prize students.

"And?" Janice prompted.

"Yes, right. Well, the Chinese got the idea that the best way to produce cubic boron arsenide without impurities was to start with the purest ingredients. They decided to go up into space and collect boron there. They invented a sort of scooper satellite and loaded it with diamonds, Earth's purist form of carbon, and launched it into the Van Allen Belts, those doughnut-shaped rings of cosmic rays trapped in orbit by the deflective action of Earth's magnetic field. They hoped that as the satellite was bombarded by cosmic rays to literally create pure boron from the cosmic ray nuclei collisions with the carbon atoms, neatly pouched inside their satellite."

"So that's the meteor we found?" Tisha asked.

Janice nodded. "The satellite misfired on its return from orbit and ended up where you found it. Awkward for the Chinese. They hoped the U.S. would consider it unimportant space junk and ignore it. All the Chinese could do was send a backdoor request to the U.S. for its return, probably with an apology for endangering U.S. citizenry, and so on."

"So the Navy sent Sweiger to find it?" Eagle Feather asked. "But why the secrecy? Why didn't they helicopter him right to the site?"

"That's what we couldn't understand," Janice said, "until we learned about Alset Industries and their interest in boron. Alset owns a series of satellites, ostensibly to provide signals for their communication devices around the globe but which are perfectly capable of spying."

"So they could have noticed the errant landing of the Chinese super scooper," Zack said.

"Yes, and probably already knew something about its purpose," Janice said. She paused. "Most people don't realize there is a new global order. Global corporations like Alset Industries have grown economically powerful enough to take their place in that order and compete with entire countries. In fact, a consortium of global industries could one day rule the world. Anyway, Alset Industries saw their opportunity to steal the Chinese technology from the satellite and stay even in the effort to produce pure cubic boron arsenide."

"So it was Alset Industries that sent in Sweiger?" Tisha asked.

"We think so. We found that a certain Navy admiral in Washington has invested heavily in Alset and may be under their thumb. We seized his communication records and found enough to know he is an old friend of the Command Chief at China Lake Naval Air Weapons Station, Simon Barroff. We think the admiral arranged with Barroff for Sweiger to go there on behalf of Alset."

Zack's head was spinning. "Then who sent Maria? Was it the Chinese?"

"That's our best guess," Janice said. "The Chinese must have learned of Alset Industries' plan, probably through their army of hackers, and sent the assassin Maria to make sure Sweiger never reached his goal."

"Then who hired me to find Sweiger?" Eagle Feather asked. "The U.S. Navy signed my check for all the good it did me."

"We think Commander Barroff could also be under the thumb of Alset Industries through this admiral in Washington."

Tisha pouted. "I don't think Simon Barroff was involved. I think once he saw what was happening, he did everything he could to stop it. He even saved our lives."

Janice gave a sympathetic nod.

"Who stopped payment on my check, if not Barroff?" Eagle Feather asked.

Zack looked thoughtfully at Eagle Feather. "Maybe Barroff didn't want the U.S. Navy paying for a service ordered by some other entity. Or maybe he had a change of conscience. He seemed upset by what was happening and most interested in keeping his base clear of such matters, even to the extent of closing it down completely."

Janice smiled at Zack. "It would be nice to think that, but we can only guess his motives."

Eagle Feather was not satisfied. "If all this is true, and Maria was working for the Chinese, why would they send her to kill me? "

"Maybe they didn't," Janice said. "Think about Alset Industries' position. They've sent in Sweiger, but he disappears, possibly kidnapped. They can't let anyone find out they sent him. At that point, the only thing they can do is eliminate anyone who knew anything about him, and that includes you."

"Okay. But Maria? She—"

"Let me finish," Janice said. "I think the assassin you killed on the mesa worked for Alset. But suppose Maria was tracking him, not you? She never shot at you, did she?"

Zack glanced at Janice in admiration. Beauty and intelligence! She had it all.

Grinning at Eagle Feather, he said, "She's right! Maria was clever enough to let you kill the Alset agent instead of doing it herself." He chuckled. "But she left you that taunting message."

Eagle Feather didn't reply.

"I'm guessing the man Maria killed at the impact crater also worked for Alset Industries," Tisha said. "Is that right?"

Janice nodded. "I'm sure that was another attempt by Alset Industries to get information and samples from the satellite."

"Then Maria ambushed us in the truck and tried to steal the samples Rackwell had taken," Zack said. "I'm sure that would have been an unexpected bonus for her Chinese clients."

"But her attempt failed because of Eagle Feather," Tisha said with a grateful glance at the Navajo. "And you, of course," she added, looking at Janice.

Janice nodded her acknowledgment.

"Who sent the man who killed my brother?" The question came from Esther. She was seated near the door to the kitchen.

Everyone looked at her in surprise. They'd forgotten she was among them once she'd returned with tea for everyone.

"Ah, yes, the bartender," Janice said. "Again, my best guess is Alset Industries. Your brother was a constant thorn in their side, not just here in the valley but beyond. It makes sense they'd have placed an agent near him to keep the company informed of his whereabouts." She sent a sad glance to Esther. "I think killing him at that moment was opportunistic for them."

Janice paused and looked at everyone in turn. "I remind you that everything we've discussed here is top secret. As I told Zack, after we received the satellite samples, we sent them to our lab for analysis. They were since removed. Only a handful of the highest offices in our government could have authorized that. It happened a short time before your brother died."

Zack studied Janice's face. "Do you think Alset influenced a very high official to help them obtain the samples and simultaneously planned to kill the rest of us?"

Janice spoke with quiet intensity. "We cannot underestimate the power and audacity of the CEO of a global company with assets greater than many countries. I have little doubt that Alset Industries' CEO, Nolan Kusum, has finally acquired the satellite samples and at the same time attempted to eliminate those most connected to and knowledgeable of his actions."

Everyone's eyes were on Janice. The sheer scale and brutality of that scenario shocked even Zack.

"But you still have the data from the samples," Eagle Feather said, casting a shrewd eye toward Janice.

"Yes, I do." A twitch of a smile touched her face, but she said no more.

Everyone sipped tea in silence.

Tisha stirred. "I have a four o'clock flight home," she said. "Can I go without fearing someone will blow my plane up?"

Janice laughed. "I think you'll be fine now. We have officially initiated investigations into Alset Industries with the support of the National Security Office. Alset won't make any more attempts on your lives now."

"And China?"

"China will pretend absolutely nothing ever happened."

"They can't be happy," Tisha remarked. "Both Alset and the U.S. have the results of their satellite experiment, but the Chinese do not."

"I wouldn't worry about China," Eagle Feather remarked. "They've probably already hacked into the lab results."

Everyone laughed at that, although no one doubted the possibility.

Janice stood, looking weary but pleased. She spread her arms wide. "Go home, everybody," she said.

EPILOGUE

Zack and Eagle Feather met for lunch and a beer a month later at Katie's Cafe in Elk Wells, Navajo Nation. The Navajo had a long, thin box wrapped with brown paper he placed on the table between them. A postal stamp with a return address in the Grand Duchy of Luxembourg was on it.

Zack raised questioning eyebrows.

Eagle Feather opened the box and folded back the tissue paper covering the item within. It was a knife.

"That's your knife," Zack said.

"Yes, it's my knife. Maria polished and returned it to me. It arrived in the post this morning."

"The same...?"

"Yes. It's the knife I threw at Maria at the Poolside Cafe."

"She kept it and mailed it back to you!"

The Navajo nodded. "There is a note."

He handed a small folded piece of plain paper to Zack.

The note was typed and unsigned. It read, "Navajo 2, Chemehuevi 0. This time."

"So I did nick her with a lucky shot that day! I thought so."

"I have a question for you about Maria," Zack said. "I can understand her miraculous ability to escape seemingly impossible situations unscathed. But can you tell me how she transported Sweiger's body from where he disappeared all the way to Desolation Canyon? And at the same time, returned the Humvee?"

"That is two questions," Eagle Feather said. "Last question first. I suspect she charmed the motor pool man into assisting in the return of the Humvee. He died later, of course."

"And the first question?"

"It is true," Eagle Feather said. 'There is much about Maria that is hard to believe. But after all, she is a Chemehuevi Runner."

"The legendary messengers of the Mojave Desert who could run all the way from the Colorado River to the Pacific Coast and were reputed to have the ability to fly," Zack said.

"Yes. As was Maria's father and his father before him."

"She flew him there, then?"

Eagle Feather eyed Zack without answering and drank from his beer.

"Of course, Alset Industries could have experimental aircraft we know nothing about," Zack said.

"You can lead a White Man to the water but can not make him drink."

Zack grinned.

"I have a question for you, White Man. I have heard no news about investigations into Alset Industries. The newspapers reported the shootings at the Poolside Cafe as the actions of a random racist shooter. Brett Rackwell's death was a driving accident, according to reports. And there has been no mention of any of the other deaths that happened. Do you have any new information about any of it?"

Zack shook his head. "No. It is all above my pay grade."

"Even though you were involved and your life endangered."

Zack nodded. "You know how this works. You've been through it with me before. If I had an ordinary boss, we would not have learned as much as we did."

The Navajo grunted. "There is a legal system that cannot touch powerful people. There are laws for some but not for others. The old ways of my people, Maria's people, Esther's people were better."

"You may be right, old friend. But when have humans not fought one another? When has there not been thirst or hunger? When has there not been prejudice?"

"Here, right now, at this moment," Eagle Feather said, lifting his glass.

FINI

WHEN THE WEST WAS SIMPLE

Not Just For Kids!

"If you like classic Westerns reminiscent of Jack Schaefer and Zane Grey, you will like this novel. It is a fun read." *Amazon Reviewer*

FROM R LAWSON GAMBLE

The <u>JOHNNY ALIAS</u> *series*

JOHNNY AND THE KID

JOHNNY AND THE PREACHER

JOHNNY AND THE COMANCHE

Available At Amazon.com

www.ingramcontent.com/pod-product-compliance
Lightning Source LLC
Chambersburg PA
CBHW050715180626
46814CB00002B/442